CRYSTAL

REBECCA LISLE

For Ishbel McLaren

First published in 2010 by
Andersen Press Limited
20 Vauxhall Bridge Road
London SW1V 2SA
www.andersenpress.co.uk

Text Copyright © Rebecca Lisle, 2010
Illustrations Copyright © Rebecca Lisle, 2010
Cover illustration © Paul Hess, 2010

British Library Cataloguing in Publication Data available.

ISBN 978 1 84939 059 0

Printed and bound in Great Britain by
CPI Bookmarque, Croydon CR0 4TD

1

The Lake in the Glass Hills

Questrid didn't mean to spy on Greenwood – it just happened.

He had come across a trail of snow beazle paw prints and was following them, hoping to catch a glimpse of the rare creature, when he found freshly made *man* prints in the snow.

Who else could be here, so far up the mountain?

He smiled to himself. The day had been perfect with a clear sky and the sun sparkling like diamonds on the snow. And now it was *more* perfect. He could have fun tracking those foot prints.

He saw a flash of leaf-green between the trees. He recognised that colour, it was Greenwood's jacket! That was odd! What was *he* doing up in the Glass Hills? Greenwood was a very private man. He hardly ever left home. Mostly he worked in the Root Room carving wood or else reading in the library. What could he be up to?

If Questrid followed him, was it spying?

Then before Questrid could decide, Greenwood vanished. That made up his mind! Spying or not, he couldn't resist the mystery. Pulling his woolly hat firmly down over his curly hair, he sprinted after him.

The trail of footsteps led him straight to the snow covered mountainside. Greenwood had gone *through* the rock!

No. Now that he had reached the spot he could see there was a gap. The giant rocks overlapped, one in front of the other, leaving a narrow zigzag track between them.

Puzzled, he followed the path, wanting to know where Greenwood had gone.

A minute later he was through the concealed passageway. He stopped; amazed at what he saw. Hidden away, enclosed by steep icy cliffs, was a strange circular lake. It was about a hundred paces wide and as perfectly round as a vast plate. The lake was frozen. It was pearly white, all except the very centre, which had melted and was a vivid turquoise blue.

Greenwood was striding over the ice towards that blue patch. Questrid hung back out of sight and watched.

As Greenwood neared the melted ice he walked more tentatively, arms held wide to help him balance – like a man walking the tightrope. When he reached the water he stopped. He took something from his pocket and held it up briefly. Questrid could see that it was the size and shape of an egg. He was sure he'd seen the object before, but didn't know exactly what it was.

Then Greenwood did two strange things. First he kissed the egg object. Second he threw it into the water – so fiercely that Questrid heard the *plunk* sound from where he stood. *Plunk, plunky, plunky,* it echoed round the walls. Water droplets sprayed up and sparkled, making tiny rainbows in the sun.

Greenwood leaned over the meltwater and stared into it as if he could see something, or was hoping to see something. He stayed hunched and expectant like that for about ten minutes before at last coming back. Quickly Questrid dived behind the largest boulder and crouched there, trembling with guilt and worry. The noise of Greenwood's feet crunching over ice and snow grew closer and Questrid's heartbeat raced faster.

Suddenly Greenwood was right beside him, passing close enough to touch. Questrid took a nervous peek at him from behind the boulder as he went by. Greenwood's thin long face was so still and pale it might have been made of ice itself. He walked with his eyes focused on something miles and miles away. He didn't even glance at Questrid but strode past and out through the gap in the rocks.

Questrid stood up and sighed with relief. Now he couldn't resist taking a look at the melted water. He stepped gingerly onto the frozen lake. The ice near the shore felt solid beneath his boots, but as he got closer to the middle the ice creaked and groaned as if he were hurting it. A couple of really sharp cracks and a tearing sound made him stop about two paces from the turquoise pool.

3

The melted ice formed a perfect circle of water within the perfect circle of the lake. Oddly, the water didn't smell of fish or of rotting plants, but gave off a faint fruity smell, like squashed grapes. It looked deep, as if it went on forever and ever and ever…

He stared into its turquoise depths. Nothing. Whatever it was that Greenwood had thrown in, had sunk to the very bottom and disappeared.

2

The Lake in the Town

'Mum! Mum, where are you?' Crystal's voice echoed off the empty walls of the apartment. 'Mum!'

She checked each room then went to the doorway and peered outside into the street. She called again and again but there was no answer. The sky was grey and dirty looking: it wasn't a good time to be out.

Crystal wanted to go to the lake. She had a sudden urge to stand at the edge and watch the water ripple and lap at the shore. But first her mother had to be found.

She stared past the derelict, shattered houses and the mounds of rubble in the street. Where *was* her mother? Once before she'd disappeared like this and that time Crystal had found her at— She ran to the side of the block and peered up towards the scrawny trees fringing Lop Lake. Yes, there! A hooded figure in a long skirt slipped in and out between the tree trunks. It was difficult to see in this gloomy twilight, but who else would it be?

It had to be her mum. But what was she doing? And had their spy seen her go?

Crystal dashed back inside. The sly-ugg was on the wall near the fireplace. It was about the size of a stunted courgette, only it was grey and orange. It was watching her, of course. Its inch-long eye-stalks twisted and waved like tiny dancing snakes. It must have seen her mum leave but Crystal could stop it from seeing more, or at least distract it.

She dropped a handful of fresh loffseed leaves in front of it. The sly-ugg always gobbled up loffseed leaves, so she thought they were its favourite. Quickly she raked up the coals in the fireplace and tossed a cup of water onto them. Smoke and steam puffed into the room. She heard a tiny wheeze from the sly-ugg, a minuscule cough. Serve it right. She heaped the coal dust from the bottom of the bucket onto the fire and waved her arms so the smoke rose up. Now the sly-ugg wouldn't see her go. It was against the law to leave the sly-ugg – it had to accompany them everywhere. But not now, Crystal thought. Something odd was happening with her mum up at the lake and she didn't want the sly-ugg to see.

She ran to the lake, jumping broken walls and stones and clattering over the sheets of corrugated iron that lay like giant playing cards along the path. She stopped beside a tree; it was a sick, warped thing with hardly any greenery, but still she breathed in the scent of sap and leaves greedily. She imagined the little tree responding to her touch, bending towards her rather than away. Crystal could watch her mother from here.

Lop Lake was perfectly round, as if someone had set down a plate and drawn round it before filling it with dingy water. Twisted bars of metal poked out from the surface like the bones of drowned animals; oil swirled on the surface. It was so grimy and stinking that no one else came here, not even the frogs. But Crystal did.

And now here was her mother, looking taller, nobler than Crystal had ever seen her before. She'd thrown back her hood and her white-blonde hair shimmered in the dull light. She was standing at the lake edge looking *through* the rubbish, staring *through* the dirty brown water. A sudden ripple of warm wind and the steely sky seemed to tense, like the air before a thunderstorm.

Crystal's skin felt electric. Something was going to happen: she shivered with anticipation.

A bubble rose and burst in the centre. A ripple formed, then another, concentric circles frilled outwards.

Something was coming...

There it was! Something round, something no bigger than an egg, flew out of the lake and soared into the sky. Droplets scattered, shimmering in a sun that wasn't there. The object rose up and arced towards Crystal's mum. She caught it, hugged it to her chest and then immediately turned and ran back to their block.

She *ran*. Crystal had never seen her mum run before. Or look so lively, so *alive*.

Crystal quickly stepped up to the lake's edge herself.

She loved the smell of the water and breathed it in deeply. She could smell *behind* the rotten leaves and oil; she could smell the water itself, like the scent of a just-bitten-into crisp apple. The scent of water was the scent of life to her. Perhaps her mother felt that too.

The grey water in Lop Lake looked as if it went down and down forever and ever. Perhaps it did. She peered into the water's depths but the lake held no answers to her mother's odd behaviour.

The smoke had cleared by the time Crystal got back home. She hoped the sly-ugg hadn't noticed her mother's absence. It had slithered along the wall and was coiled up like a pale dog turd on a shelf close by her mum. Hateful thing. Theirs was particularly ugly: orange, dotted with grey spots and a covering of mucus and slime. It was coated with a thin layer of soot, now, too. It was watching Crystal's mum so intently that its eyes were bulging like balloons on the end of their stalks.

And well it might! Her mum was shining, glowing! As if a spotlight were focused on her. She was drumming her foot on the hearth: tap, tap, *pound*, tap, tap, and *pound*. Icicle, their black kitten, clung on to her lap as he was jogged up and down. He looked worried.

Most days her mother sat by the hearth, dreamy and vague. On good days she made medicines. On troubled days she painstakingly chipped away at a lump of wood, a sculpture, though she never said what it was going to be. There were several odd-shaped chunks of wood in the apartment carved by her mother. One, which looked like a sort of house with a door and windows, was currently used to wedge open the kitchen window in the summer. Her mum seemed to drift around in a secret pool of quietness, never looking truly alive. But now, now she was sparkling!

'Mum, what is it? What's the matter?' Crystal asked. She looked around for the thing that had flown out of the lake, but saw no sign of it.

Her mother took Crystal's hand and squeezed it. 'Is there something wrong with me, darling?' Her blue eyes blazed. 'Something the matter?'

'Yes. No! You went up to Lop Lake. What was that thing you caught? Where is it?'

Crystal sensed the tiniest movement as the sly-ugg uncurled a little more and stretched out its eye-stalks to catch all they said. She turned her back on it.

'I don't know what you're talking about. I'm very well,' her mum said. 'I am much, much better. I know that in the end, we will get back. We will!' She threw herself back in her chair. 'The water was clear. Clear as *glass*.'

The Towners said Crystal's mum, Effie, was crazy, but that wasn't true. She was different, that was all. Silent, thoughtful and . . . different. And if the Towners thought she was a little mad, that didn't stop them from buying her remedies, lotions and poultices because there was little in the way of medicine in the Town and Effie's stuff worked. Plus, while Morton Grint, the Town leader, treated her as if she were special, she was safe.

Like Crystal, Effie was blonde with fair skin and large blue eyes. Crystal knew her mum was beautiful but the Towners preferred dark hair and dark eyes.

The other thing that made Effie different was that she remembered little of the past years and nothing of her life before arriving in the Town. All that Crystal knew of her past she had gleaned from others. She knew that they had arrived some ten or so years before, but no one knew where from or how. She had been told that at first Effie refused to speak of where she came from, then she was unable to remember. Her past had vanished.

Crystal longed to talk to someone about the extraordinary change in her mum's behaviour, but there was no one she trusted. Stella was her only close friend but because her father was an Elder, a member of Grint's inner circle, Crystal certainly couldn't tell *her*.

'What subjects are you choosing to do for Final-Sit exams?' Stella asked as she and Crystal walked back from school the following day. It was their first chance to talk because although they went to the same school, Crystal had to sit at the back where her white-blonde hair couldn't offend anyone.

'None. I'm no good at schoolwork. You know I'm not. I'll fail everything and end up working in the rationing block handing out food,' Crystal said. 'I won't reach Final-Sits.'

'Oh, Crystal, don't say that!'

'It's true. As long as I don't get sent out to the mines, that's all I care about.' She unwrapped a Minty Moment and sucked on it hard. 'I'd hate the mines. I'd hate to work in the mines. I'd hate that!'

Secretly Crystal longed to escape the Town, to go over the Wall, past the mines and everything dirty and grey and falling down to – well, she didn't know where. But to wherever she belonged, and she knew it wasn't here.

'Others like me,' she went on. 'I mean people who look different – outsiders, orphans – they are banished to the mines.' Crystal shivered. 'I really wonder why Mum and I have never been sent there.'

'Effie's special,' Stella said. 'Everyone, specially Grint, Bless and Praise his Name, knows that.'

Crystal could never quite tell whether Stella meant such comments kindly or not. She thought carefully before she spoke again.

'I was thinking that instead of doing my Finals, Mum and I might try and get a permit to leave,' Crystal said quietly.

Stella looked at her sharply. 'Crystal! That's like saying you don't like it here! Or you don't admire our leader. That's almost treason.'

Crystal kicked some broken glass out of her path. 'We don't belong. We'll never belong. We have to take the sly-ugg every week to Raek. Mum has to see Grint—'

'Bless and Praise his Name!' Stella said quickly.

'But *you* don't!' Crystal said. 'You don't have a sly-ugg. You like it here, you belong here, but we—'

'Shh! Look, there *is* Raek!' said Stella.

'Wonder what nasty business he's on,' Crystal whispered.

'Good afternoon, Raek.' Stella nodded politely at him and nudged Crystal to do the same. Crystal's nod was so tiny as not to be seen.

Raek sailed past with hardly a glance at them.

'Pompous twit!' Crystal said under her breath.

'Hush! Don't! Raek is very important. You must be polite to him, Crystal. Please do try. If you tried to fit in a bit better, maybe you would.'

'I can't be polite to him. When I take Mum to the house to see Grint—'

'Bless and Praise his Name!' Stella hissed.

' – Raek's always so horrid.'

'You don't realize how lucky you are. I've never even been inside the House, though Dad has of course.'

'What does Grint want to see Mum for? As if she's a criminal!'

'Our leader knows best,' Stella said. 'We're well looked after. Some people would love the chance to go and see him like you do. And there are only about ten families with a sly-ugg in the whole Town. Honestly, you don't know how lucky you are. Isn't having a sly-ugg rather an honour?'

'No! Are you mad? It watches Mum all day while I'm at school, then it watches me when I get home. We have to keep it with us all the time. It's a spy, that's all. What does *he* want to see Mum for, Stella? She's ill. I think she's getting worse. I worry. There's something...' She was thinking back to her mum's odd behaviour at Lop Lake, her new spirit.

Stella played with her black hair and smiled blankly. She didn't *want* to know. It wasn't normal, so she did not want to know, but Crystal couldn't leave the subject alone.

'After each visit to *him* she seems worse. *More* confused.'

'I'm sure you're wrong,' Stella said. 'Anyway, Effie can't be that confused because she makes good medicine, doesn't she? She cured Mr Bolton's leg ulcers, I heard. Her medicines are famous; everyone uses her lotions... Although Dad told me some cousin – I think her name was Annie Scott – was given stuff by your mum and now she's worse!'

'Annie Scott? I didn't know she was your relation... The doctor couldn't do anything for her so Mum's medicine was the last resort.'

Stella fluffed up her long black hair and quickly changed the subject.

'My mum said that Effie's mind is so empty, you know, with her not having any old memories, that whatever Grint, Bless and Praise his Name, asks her, she gives him a clear answer. And the other thing I heard someone say – though I don't know if this is true – is that Grint, Bless and Praise his Name, might have come from the same place as Effie. He's not quite the same as us Towners either, really, is he? He doesn't have blonde hair like you, but you know what I mean?' Stella looked at Crystal carefully but Crystal was too busy thinking about this idea to notice.

'Where did Grint come from?' Crystal asked.

'I don't know... I've never thought about it... I thought Effie might have said... Anyway, listen, a skweener carried off a guard from the Wall last night!'

Crystal shivered. 'I still have nightmares that a skweener will come over the Wall and get me.'

'Me too! This one was green and had spiked wings and a long tail,' Stella said. 'It swooped down and grabbed this poor man. It had talons like massive hooks, Dad said – and carried him away. And you know we won those tickets to go out and see the mines? Well, what if we get attacked by a skweener when we go out of the gate? I'm scared! You don't really want to get a permit and leave, do you? I'd miss you. And it's not safe out there.'

'I don't feel safe *in* here.'

'Don't feel safe?' Stella cried. 'But this is the Town! This is our home!'

'Home for you, Stella, but even your dad – well, I've heard him in the Square. He sometimes says things – not against Grint – well, not exactly, but he challenges him—'

'Dad is loyal,' Stella said firmly, ending the discussion.

If Crystal and her mum got a permit to leave, she would find out what was on the other side of the Wall. Surely it couldn't be worse than here. Maybe they could travel miles and miles and find . . .

'What are you dreaming about, Crystal?'

'Nothing. We've got to go to the House tonight,' Crystal said. 'And Mum is—'

'Yes?'

No, she didn't dare tell her what had happened at Lop Lake. 'Nothing.'

3

In the Marble Mountains

Questrid retrieved his sledge from the shelter of the furzz trees by the split in the mountain wall and pointed it down the hill towards home – Spindle House.

'Yahoo!' he cried as he pushed off. 'Yahoo!'

Sledging *downhill* was so brilliant it was worth all the effort of lugging it *uphill*. He shot down like a bullet. Snow flew up around him, the cold wind whipped his cheeks, nipped his nose and made his eyes water. Bliss!

From a distance Spindle House looked like a giant tree; it was only when you saw the smoking chimneys and the little windows that you realized it was a house. The rooms in the trunk were shaped like slices of cake with the pointed ends cut off, and upstairs, inside the giant branches, the rooms were strange wobbly shapes.

Questrid paused for a moment on the top of the last rise and stared at the tree. He picked out Copper's dark window. Like him, she was from both the Rock and Wood tribes, so they understood each other, though it was Wood that predominated in her character and Rock and Stone in his. She and her parents were away. He missed them. Greenwood's window was at the very top, far away from the rest of the family. Typical. And over there was the stable building on the other side of the courtyard where Questrid spent most of his time. Home.

Questrid tipped the sledge down the rise and sped on smoothly through the gateway, stopping right inside the walled courtyard. Good fun, but it would be better when Copper was back and they went sledging and skating together again.

The two horses, Thunder and Lightning, leaned out over the stable door and snorted a greeting at him. He patted their noses and stroked their ears. 'Good fellows. Good boys.' Questrid propped his sledge up inside the porch by the back door and went in. Opening the door set off a draft of wind through the kitchen and sent birds rising in a flurry of wings. They burst into a noisy chatter and then settled again just as quickly. Silver, the great dog-like wolf, came up and sniffed him with interest. Questrid patted her head.

Oriole, the housekeeper, was cooking soup; her partner, Robin, was sitting at the table cradling a bird in his hands. Other birds were perched on the dresser and backs of chairs, while more flew in and out of an opening in the window.

'This thrush has broken a wing feather,' Robin told Questrid. 'I'm trying to mend it.'

A large owl with brilliant sparky round eyes was perched on the back of the rocking chair. It stared at

Questrid haughtily. 'Twit twoo!'

'Twit you are too,' Questrid said with a laugh. 'Is Greenwood back yet?'

'He is!' Oriole said, wiping her hands down her apron. 'And he's gone and got himself a fever! You should have seen him when he came in! Eyes glittering and cheeks on fire. I wanted him to go straight to bed, but he wouldn't. He was muttering on and on about something... I don't know.'

'Where is he?'

'Guess,' Robin said with a chuckle.

'In the Root Room?' Questrid said.

'Yes.'

'Go tell him dinner's nearly ready, will you?' Oriole said.

'OK.' Questrid went towards the kitchen door. 'It'll be good when the others are back, won't it?'

'I hope it hasn't been too boring being left with us,' Oriole said.

Questrid hugged her. Oriole was so tiny that her head only reached his chest. 'Of course not! I love you!' he said.

A narrow staircase spiralled down below the house to the Root Room. It was an underground space where the family worked carving and sculpting. The ceiling and walls were formed from a network of roots from the giant Spindle tree above.

'Hello! Hello! Greenwood?' Questrid called out. 'Oriole says dinner's nearly ready.'

To his amazement, Greenwood spun round and glared at Questrid furiously. 'No!' Greenwood yelled. He jumped up from his workbench and threw down his chisel. 'No!' He threw down his spectacles and tugged at his hair as if he wanted to pull it out. 'I simply can't bear it!' he shouted. 'No!'

Questrid was shocked, frozen to the spot. 'Greenwood?' he said softly. 'What's the matter?'

'Ahh haa!' Greenwood cried, stabbing a finger fiercely at Questrid. 'It was *you*!'

'Me? What?' Questrid felt the blood rush hotly to his cheeks. Greenwood *had* seen him at the lake.

'Are you any relation to Grint? You must be! You're a Rocker. You've Stone in your bones. You're his cousin, are you? You can't deny it!'

Questrid backed away. 'Greenwood! It's *me*, Questrid.' His voice trembled. How could Greenwood say these things? 'Who's Grint? What's the matter?'

'What? Who?' Greenwood tottered and blinked. 'What? Oh! It *is* you, Questrid! Questrid, my dear boy!' He sat down heavily. 'Thank my stars. I thought for a moment... when you came... There are forces at work, evil forces and Grint is behind it all. The lake! There was water, oh, my stars! The ice melted and there was water. I saw it. I saw it. I must get on with my work. I'm carving a handle, Questrid. A handle, because the handle will turn and when it's turned, the door will open. Doors shut things out. You do understand?'

Questrid gulped. 'Yes,' he lied. 'Yes.'

'There's a glimmer of hope, but that makes it so much worse. Hope. It's the last thing you want. When that's gone, it's all gone. Easier without it: easier with nothing.

18

I must get on with the carving. Don't stop me. You mustn't try and stop me!'

Greenwood had flipped! Gone mad!

Questrid backed out and ran to get help. But although Robin, Oriole and he went down to the Root Room to try and persuade Greenwood to come upstairs and be looked after, he refused. Nothing they could do or say that afternoon would make him leave the workroom or his chunks of wood.

Questrid loved Spindle House but he never wanted to stay in there longer than he had to; it was too woody. He certainly couldn't sleep there. The massive branches of the vast Spindle tree creaked and bent in the wind and every plank and joist sighed and squeaked as it moved. He preferred his nights to be still and so he had a large bedroom above the stables. The sound of the horses' hoofs shuffling on the straw-covered paving stones and their heavy breathing soothed him.

Questrid was exhausted after his strange talk with Greenwood and then trying to bargain with him to leave the cellar. He felt the need to be alone in his own room. He ripped off his long scarf and hat and kicked off his boots.

The afternoon sun was slanting in through the roof windows. It was usually one of his favourite times of day, but now he was worrying about Greenwood.

Questrid had been planning to design a sculpture of two snow beazles rolling around in a tangle of legs and tails; it would make a good present for his mother, Ruby. Now, because of Greenwood, he hadn't the heart to start it.

He opened up his notebook and flicked through the pages of designs.

Suddenly he stopped.

'Pheeew!' He looked from his design to the shelf where he kept his carvings: back to the book, up to the shelf.

He thought he knew what it was that Greenwood had thrown into the lake.

4

A Visit to Grint

Lop Lake had done something to Effie.

She cleaned the stove and swept the floors. She began digging in the space behind the apartment where they grew turnips and potatoes, saying, 'We must have a pond. Running water. A river would be good.' Crystal brought water from the well. She set the bucket beside her mother so that in the evening she could run her fingers through it. She liked the sound it made, she said.

'What came out of Lop Lake? Where did you put it?' Crystal asked her time and again. She'd looked for the object in their rooms but needed time on her own to search properly. 'It looked like a stone or an egg or something...'

'I don't know,' her mother would say with a smile, 'but it was wonderful by the water, wasn't it?'

'Do you remember catching something?'

'No. Did I? I don't remember.'

It was impossible! And now they were seeing Grint that night. How would Crystal explain if he noticed the change in Effie?

She handed her mum a long black scarf. It had become their custom to cover their hair in an attempt not to draw attention to it when they went out.

'No.' Effie pushed the scarf away. 'Why should I hide my hair? I never used to have to do such miserable things. I want something lively – blue or gold or silver – to wear! We never wore black at home.'

Home.

Crystal had never heard her mention 'home' before. She glanced towards the sly-ugg. Its eyes were closed but that didn't mean it wasn't listening.

'What do you mean, "we never wore black", Mum?' Crystal whispered. She couldn't keep the longing from her voice. 'Who's *we*? Where's *home*?'

Crystal stared into her mum's ice-blue eyes, which were gazing directly back at her. She realized with a jolt that her mum usually stared vacantly straight past her.

'I'm trapped,' Effie said, putting her hands to her throat. 'Stuck in a terrible limbo. It's like living one night years and years long but with no dreaming, no waking, no touching, no feeling. He's taken my memories. No snow! Crystal, it's like being dead. I want to see the snow.'

'I don't understand. *Snow?* I wish—'

'But I've woken up, Crystal. We must be careful. Play safe. Yes.' She looked round anxiously. 'We can fool Grint. We must not let him know... Give me that stupid bit of cloth!'

Effie deftly wrapped the black scarf around her pale hair. Usually Crystal had to do it while her mum sat like a pudding on a plate. 'I have to see his high and mighty-ship, I know. I know,' Effie rattled on. 'I should never have let him use me like this. I should have battled and oh, done anything to escape. How have I let this happen, Crystal?'

'What, Mum? I wish I could understand you.'

'This! To be caught here like a salmon in a net.'

'Mum! Hush!'

'Yes, yes, hush! The sly-ugg might hear and then Raek will hear. And Grint will hear. I know, I know, but it's too late anyway. If only I didn't have to go! Grint works in mysterious ways. What would you say Mr Grint has coursing though his veins, Crystal? Do you think he has real blood or mercury? What's in his heart? Iron, or is it marble?'

'I really don't know, I—' Crystal quickly dropped an upturned bowl over the sly-ugg. 'Whoops, how silly of me!' she cried, then aside in a fierce whisper to her mother: 'Mum! The sly-ugg! Please! You're talking treason.'

'*Treason!* Is it treason to know we're trapped here, kept against our will? But . . .' She paused, thinking. 'Is having hope worse? It might be. We must escape, Crystal. That's what we must do! Prisoners escape.'

Crystal turned away and hid her tears. Her mother was truly mad. She really was.

'Stone in his heart, Crystal,' her mum muttered. 'He is grit and gravel and hardness. Quartz in his bones.'

'Shh! Yes, Mum. Come on. We'll be late.'

Effie grasped Crystal's arm. 'You think I'm crazy. My darling, dearest daughter, I am not mad. I am so *not* mad. If something goes wrong and I don't speak like this again; if I seem to forget, try and remember this moment.' She looked round anxiously and gripped Crystal hard. 'I have a feeling this won't last. I don't know how to hold on to this wakefulness.'

'I'll try to remember,' Crystal said. 'I'll try and do everything you say.'

Crystal lifted the bowl off the sly-ugg. Its eye-stalks twisted and waved rapidly then it fixed her with an intense stare as if it had caught a bit of her mother's new fiery spirit. 'What's up with you?' she said. 'Sorree! Don't you like it under there? I suppose it's not your fault you're so horrid. Come on. Time for a walk.'

They had a sly-ugg carry-box for trips, made of light thin metal. It had a handle at the top and one side opened for the sly-ugg to go in and out. The opening side was made of a thin mesh so that the sly-ugg could continue spying wherever it was.

Crystal put some dandelion leaves into the carry-box and then swept the greasy creature in too. It left a trail of grey, snotty slime behind on the table.

The black kitten sat at the window and watched them go, flicking his tail backwards and forwards, blinking his green eyes.

The outlines of buildings were blurred and shadowy. One or two lights glowed through chinks of half-closed shutters. The warm wind moaned. It whistled through glass-less windows and whined like a poltergeist as it whipped round the vast empty factories and rows of abandoned houses and tall office blocks.

Grint's stone house in the Square stood in grand isolation. Two columns of granite, carved like totem poles, guarded the front door. Every time Crystal visited the House she felt compelled to look at them. She'd heard that Grint had carved the columns himself: strange faces, mountains and flying beasts. Crystal found it hard to believe that Grint's hands could ever have made anything so beautiful.

They rang the doorbell. Raek, Grint's second-in-command, opened the door. He was dressed in his habitual grey suit, his thin hair neatly greased back over his bony skull. 'Late,' he snapped. His lips were blistered and his cheeks looked sore. Crystal tried not to stare. Raek looked at them coldly, holding out his gloved hand for the carry-box. 'I'll take that.'

Crystal handed him the carry-box. They were heading through the big hall towards Grint's receiving room where Crystal usually took her mother, when Raek stopped them. He held up his narrow hand grandly. 'Wait. Grint, Bless and Praise his Name, has the Elders with him in the hall.' He pointed to the waiting room. 'Sit in there.'

He strode away, taking the sly-ugg with him.

Crystal stared after him, looking at his narrow skinny shoulders. How did he get the information out of the sly-ugg? She'd seen the sly-ugg retract its eyes and curl up into a tight little coil when Raek walked by. Whatever he did, she reckoned, it wasn't kind.

Effie sat down and started tapping her foot on the stone floor. And humming.

Crystal hushed her. There were voices coming from the hall and she wanted to hear what was being said.

' . . . There have been several incidents of sorcery,' said a man. 'Permission to ban entirely the mixing and making of love potions and the use of so-called magic stones, sir?'

'Granted!' Morton Grint's voice was unmistakable, rough and low. It always reminded Crystal of pebbles shifting and grinding against each other.

'There is a lot of medicine-making going on amongst the women,' another man said. 'Do you think we should be allowing this? Should we crack down on this nonsense? We have good doctors in Town.'

'Doctors are expensive. Only some can afford them,' John Carter, Stella's father, said.

'Maybe, but potions and herbal brews are old-fashioned and I don't think they should be used unless they're regulated.'

Several voices shouted their agreement.

'There is perhaps room for different forms of medicine,' Grint said slowly. 'Reflexology. Leeches.'

There was much muttering and shouting.

'One final point—' It was John Carter again. He was often in the Square talking loudly to anyone who would listen about Town matters. He was an Elder, a trusted member of Grint's inner circle, but he spoke out freely against Grint's policies. 'What about Barnaby Andrews? Will you explain that, Grint?'

'Yes, Barnaby!' someone called. 'How did you know

about Barnaby? He doesn't have a sly-ugg to monitor him.'

'Perhaps he should have!'

Laughter.

'There are other ways and means of knowing what's going on in my town,' Grint said. 'I heard about Barnaby plotting, found out who his accomplices were and acted accordingly.'

'Is there *nothing* anyone does that you don't know about, sir?'

They all laughed.

'Nothing!' Grint cried.

The men cheered.

The group departed, and about five minutes later Raek ushered Crystal and her mother in to Morton Grint.

Grint was sitting in a gold chair. He was rubbing the sides of his head with his thumbs as if he had a headache. He was a small, wiry man and despite being old, still had a mass of iron-grey hair like a lion's mane that he wore swept off his high forehead. His teeth, on the other hand, were very small and even and yellow. He remained seated as Crystal and her mother came in, but watched them carefully through half-closed eyes.

Two bright spots burned on Effie's cheeks as if she had a fever. She looked nervously round the room. Crystal prayed Grint wouldn't notice.

'Something has disturbed your mother, Crystal,' he said straightaway. 'She looks different.'

'I could take her home again if you want.' Crystal's heart was beating fast. She wished her mother would not pluck at the hem of her cloak like that, or tap her foot. She prayed she wouldn't say anything foolish or crazy.

'No, no,' Grint said. 'I wouldn't miss an evening with Effie for anything.'

'If you're sure?' Crystal said.

'Of course I'm sure! Go now,' Grint said. 'Come back in one hour.'

'Goodbye, Mum,' Crystal called as she went.

In fine weather, while Effie was with Grint, Crystal waited on the porch. When it was raining she sat in the waiting room. But tonight she was going to go home: it was a chance for her to find the egg thing from Lop Lake without her mother and the sly-ugg watching.

She glanced up at the purple sky: just time before dark fell completely and the night curfew began.

She ran.

Her block felt very big, very empty without her mum. She even missed the sly-ugg. At least it was another living, breathing creature. Without them, the place was echoing and dismal. Knowing there were hundreds of empty rooms above her made her skin tingle uncomfortably. She sucked a Minty Moment. She had to ration her sweets because she only had a few each week, but she did love them. They seemed to give her courage.

In the evening quiet she could hear muffled thudding and pounding from the distant mines. Grint used great wild creatures called rockgoyles to dig, as well as every poor Towner who'd ever been banished. How long before being different from everyone else meant she was sent out there too?

Crystal started her search.

She looked between the folds of Effie's few clothes in the dressing table. Nothing. She searched under the bed. She looked in the kitchen drawers and on high ledges. She didn't even know what she was looking for. It wasn't big. Not so small. The impression that it had been egg-shaped was strong in her mind. But what could that mean? *Where* could it be?

She searched everywhere. Nothing. She had to get back to the House before the hour was up. Abandoning her search, she ran.

Moon moss

5

A Visit to the Swamp

By the time Crystal was racing back to Grint's house it was almost nightfall. She slipped into the porch and steadied her breathing. The door opened immediately. Raek's spotty red face cracked into a grin. 'Terrible calamity,' he said. 'Your mother has been taken ill.'

'Oh, no! Where is she?' Crystal pushed past him recklessly. I shouldn't have brought her, she thought. She was ill, not mad. She must have had a fever and I never thought— Oh, I'm so stupid!

Grint met her in the hall. 'No need to worry, Effie's being looked after. She asked you to go and gather some moss for her. *Moon moss*. She said you'd know it.'

'But can't I see her?'

'There's no need.'

'I must!'

Grint's tongue darted out like a little snake between his lips. 'Show a bit of respect, Crystal Waters. Do try.' He sighed. 'Very well. This way.'

The receiving room was crammed with fine wooden furniture, rare in the Town, which was why Grint had it. He himself always sat on one of the wrought-iron chairs or even on the stone bench. She let her fingers drift over the back of a couch as she passed it, imagining she felt it ripple under her fingertips, responding to her touch. When they escaped, when they got home – wherever that was – she would surround herself with carved wooden furniture like this, and wooden floors and wooden walls and...

The room was empty. Why wasn't her mother in there?

Grint led her out into a wide corridor.

'Mum!'

Effie was lying on a large divan. Her face was white. Her eyes were shut. Crystal ran to her side. 'What's she doing out here?'

Grint shrugged. 'She felt faint,' he said. 'She said you'd help. Asked me to tell you to collect moon moss for her. Fresh moon moss.'

Crystal held back her tears. This was all because of what happened at the lake. 'I don't want to leave her. Can't we get a doctor?'

'We could, but she *said* she wanted moon moss. You want to do what she wants, I suppose?' Grint frowned. 'She said it grew at the swamp. It isn't some sort of witchcraft, is it? I won't allow that.'

'Moon moss? No, it's just a herb. All right. I'll go.' She turned and almost bumped into Raek, who'd quietly crept up behind them.

'Watch where you're going!' he said. He had put on an ankle-length coat and was carrying two lanterns. His frog-eyes were bulging with excitement.

He meant to go with her!

'*He* doesn't need to come,' Crystal said.

'Raek will go with you to the swamp. It's the curfew.'

'But – Oh...' What could she do? She had to accept Raek's company during the curfew because on her own she'd be arrested.

Moon moss was a tiny plant that produced small white globular flowers all over a dense mound of leaves. From a distance it looked like one giant flower glowing like moonlight. Crystal had picked some a few weeks ago for Annie Scott. And they had some at home. Surely she didn't need to go and pick fresh leaves – but if her mum had said she should...

It was now quite dark outside. The streets were deserted; no one was allowed out unless they had special permission.

Crystal walked briskly, hating having Raek jogging behind her, feeling him watching her back. She focused on the light from their swinging lanterns making their shadows lurch into vast monsters or shrink to a weird nothing. It was a novelty being out in the dark.

'Town Guard!' Raek snapped suddenly.

The sound of the Guards' boots pounding the ground had been audible for some time. Now their lanterns came into view. The light flashing off their gold buttons glittered like hundreds of watchful eyes.

'Halt! Who goes there?' the lead Guard asked. 'Papers!'

Raek flashed his identity card.

'Of course you have permission. Apologies, Mr Raek,' the lead Guard said. 'I thought I recognized you but I had to be sure.'

He glanced suspiciously at Crystal. 'Is everything all right, missy?'

'We're on business,' Raek snapped. 'Morton Grint's business.'

'Very well.'

The Town Guards' footsteps died away as they marched off. The darkness crept in again. Crystal shivered.

'You and me are not so different you know, Crystal,' Raek said. 'I have no parents and you can hardly count your mother as a proper parent, can you? And who knows who your father was? No one. I was from the outside. I learned how to adapt. I changed. You could do that too and then you could get on. You could learn to fit in and then I think being different could be an advantage. Even though you're a blonde freak. If you just showed a bit of respect towards me, Crystal... You're not natural. I think...'

Crystal pulled her cloak over her hair. '*You're* not natural,' she said under her breath.

'I don't understand why Grint, Bless and Praise his Name, hasn't locked you both up, I really don't.'

Crystal sighed. 'We don't do any harm—'

'He needs Effie, I can see that,' Raek persisted from behind her. 'He locks the door. I listen; I eavesdrop. I know she's important to him. But there's more. Some other link.' His voice was low, as if he were really talking only to himself.

They passed down a street of empty houses with corrugated steel sheets nailed up over them; and across a patch of rubble and stone to the end of the broken tarmac road. One more group of Town Guards came past and checked Raek's papers before moving off into the dark again.

'People can sleep easy in this place,' Raek muttered. 'Don't you agree, Crystal, they can sleep easy with the Guard around?'

Crystal hated the sound of their marching boots going by in the night, but she didn't say so.

'They are saying your mum's a witch. The Elders are cracking down on witchcraft, Crystal. Anything that smells like witchcraft, anything that is remotely connected to witchcraft will be dealt with harshly. If you ask me, moon moss is pretty much—'

'Mum can't remember things. Now she's ill.'

'Humph,' Raek puffed. 'I say Effie can remember *when* she has to, and *what* she has to.'

They were climbing over mounds of debris, clattering over stones and fallen bricks. Crystal tried not to listen to him. She tried to think only of her mother and of making her better.

'We haven't had a witch in the Town for years. Used to burn them long ago,' Raek went on. 'Used to put them on a stake and burn out all the sorcery and magic. Always had a black cat, they did, and *your* mother...'

Crystal swung round and glared at him. 'Shut up or—' She froze; horrified she'd dared speak to Raek like that. Stella would be furious with her. She turned away quickly.

Raek smoothed his tongue over his sore lips and did not speak for a few moments.

'Be careful. Softly, softly,' he said. 'You shouldn't talk to me like that, Crystal. I've made myself a person of consequence. Morton Grint, Bless and Praise his Name, has made me his right-hand man, and as he goes up, I go up with him. But if he goes down, well, I intend to stay up. You need to keep in my good books.'

Crystal clamped her mouth shut. She must learn to curb her sharp words. She mustn't say anything.

They walked on down the cinder path, on towards the blackness of an old factory chimney and the swamp.

The swamp – a vast expanse of black oily mud – stretched away in front of them from the derelict chimney to the distant North Gate. Half a mile of dangerous black that sucked down anything that fell in it. Nobody who had fallen in had ever been taken from it alive. An ancient wooden walkway ran across it. Crystal rested her palm on the smoothed rail and straightaway felt stronger.

Tiny mounds of green moss and lichen grew in clumps over the swamp. Small twisted trees sprang out of miniature mossy islands. Crystal believed it had to be a good place if it had trees and moon moss.

'Go on, then.' Raek gave her a push.

'Don't touch me!' She spun round angrily, almost hitting him with her lantern.

He was laughing at her. 'Not scared, are you? Witch child! Alien! Silver head!'

Crystal turned away and stepped onto the planks. They were greasy with moss and mould. 'It's slippery. Hold up your lantern, please.'

Raek backed away from the edge of the black sludge. 'It won't be strong enough for the two of us,' he muttered. 'I'll wait here.' He held up his lantern though.

Coward, Crystal thought. The walkway was strong enough to take ten men, but she didn't care, she'd rather be alone.

The moon appeared between the clouds and for a second it was reflected in the oily expanse, making the black surface appear like molten silver. The mud sighed and heaved and shifted around her, releasing nose-tingling sulphurous smells.

Moon moss. Moon moss. She knew exactly where it was: just where a thin young oak tree branched right over the walkway. She set off, treading very carefully on the slippery boards.

She hadn't gone far when she heard something.

'Raek? What was that noise?' She hesitated, listening. There was the sound of something moving, shifting.

'I didn't hear anything,' Raek called from the edge of the swamp.

Crystal shrugged and went on.

Each step had to be taken carefully. The boards were slippery and she only had one hand free to hold the rail.

How quiet it was. How much darker it grew as she got further from Raek with only the light from her own lantern to guide her.

Again she heard the strange shuffling noise. She stopped and turned. Raek was still there, just a dot of light now, but still there.

She walked on, swinging her lantern from left to right. The mud glittered and sparkled in the light; little swamp creatures went skittering away into the shadows.

Thud! Flap! What was *that*?

She stopped, holding her breath. There *was* something on the walkway. She listened intently. It was on the planks behind her! Now it wasn't so much that she could hear it, but *feel* it; the wooden walkway was vibrating as something came towards her.

Raek. He must have changed his mind. He was following – but the footsteps were so heavy...

Crystal swallowed. She turned slowly, afraid of what she'd see.

The light had gone! Raek had disappeared.

'Raek! Raek!'

Behind her all was darkness. Or was there something darker, blacker, coming along the walkway? It *had* to be Raek – who else could it be? His lantern had burned out. He'd got scared, or lonely... It had to be Raek. But she knew it wasn't.

The planks were shuddering. Something was thudding on the walkway. The wood was pulsing! The footsteps were getting stronger and heavier. Thumping. Something was *thumping* along towards her. Something much heavier than Raek...

She could hear the sound of feet, or was it paws? *Bedum, bedum*, they were drumming on the wood. *Click click*, something scratched the wood. *Swoosh, whoosh*, something heavy brushed over the planks.

Crystal looked quickly over her shoulder. Just a glimpse

was enough. It was a skweener! Its head was down low, wings held close to its side, long tail thrashing from side to side. Its eyes gleamed red. A terrible low, skweening cry burst from its open jaws.

Crystal screamed. And ran. 'Help!'

The walkway swayed from side to side, the lantern spluttered.

Her worst nightmare – a skweener!

'Help!'

The creature was almost upon her when she felt leaves brush her face – the tree! She dropped the lantern and somehow it landed upright. The flame flickered then steadied. She was up the tree in an instant, hooking her legs over a branch and pulling herself up.

The skweener thundered into the light. She could see the whites of its eyes, the curl of its yellow nostrils, scales glinting on its sinewy neck. It was so close below her she could smell its breath, ashy and hot and stinking of rotten meat.

It lumbered past, then hesitated . . .

'Skweeeeen!'

It couldn't see her. But it could smell her.

It lifted its snout and sniffed the air, pinpointed where she was and tried to spin round to head back. But the planks were as slippery as ice. The skweener's feet slithered as it turned, claws ripping at the wood, and it crashed against the rail. The rail snapped like a matchstick and the skweener tumbled into the swamp. *Splat!* like a giant wooden spoon hitting batter.

'Skweeeeen! Skweeeeen!'

The scream was terrible; it chilled Crystal to the centre of her being and made her hair stand on end. Shivering, she clung more tightly to her tree.

The skweener was stuck. It began thrashing against the mud, beating its wings and swirling its tail round in a desperate attempt to get free. The more it struggled and writhed, the deeper into the swamp it sank. It was a horrible thing to witness. 'Sorry, sorry,' she told it while she squeezed her eyes shut and blocked off her ears. 'Sorry.'

A cold sweat covered her body. She was sobbing silently, trying not to see, trying not to hear. She felt her grasp weakening and knew she'd fall at any moment. She stayed on the branch as long as she could, then finally her fingers lost their hold and she slithered down. Her legs collapsed and she crumpled in a heap on the walkway, weeping.

The skweener was barely moving now. It was covered in mud; even its gleaming eyes were blacked out. It was doomed.

At last it was quiet – except for a few bubbles slowly erupting on the slimy surface.

She opened her eyes and stared at the mud where she thought she could still see the shape of the dead skweener. That could so easily have been me, she thought.

6
The Acorn Holder

Questrid stared at his drawing in the design book:

Acorn Holder

It was an acorn – a little smaller than a chicken's egg – sitting in its knobbly cup. He had made it from a solid chunk of green marble. One end of the marble had flecks of darker green and brown in it and he had used that to form the eggcup. The other part of the marble had lines in it like wood grain, which had been perfect for the acorn itself. The acorn nut unscrewed from the cup base and both were hollow so that something could be hidden inside it, something like a slip of curled-up paper, or a trinket.

Questrid had finished carving and polishing it only last week. The screw mechanism didn't turn smoothly yet, but with a little more work it would. Copper said it was a wooden thing made of stone and therefore brilliant – like him!

He had put the acorn holder on his window ledge.

Now it wasn't there.

Perhaps it had rolled off. He began to search. There was dust under the bed, a couple of socks, spiders, but no acorn holder. He checked everywhere: in the chest of drawers, his boxes of tools, amongst his books... It had disappeared.

Questrid stared out of the window towards the Glass Hills.

He was certain. Greenwood had chucked his acorn holder into the lake.

7

Something's Not Right

Crystal's pounding heart slowly stilled. Her breathing grew calmer. She could not take her eyes from the muddy swamp.

Was the skweener truly dead? Could it still rise up and get her? She wanted to turn and run, but for a long while she did not dare move. At last she convinced herself that the skweener was really no longer a threat and she began to breathe more easily.

Her mother. Moon moss. She needed moon moss. She'd almost forgotten it in her terror, and there it was on the other side of the walkway. It was gleaming pearly white and reassuringly normal. Crystal knelt down and plucked at it with boneless fingers; she could hardly tear the spongy leaves. She pushed what she gathered into her pocket and picked up the lantern and headed back.

No Raek.

Coward! Crystal didn't wait to find out what had happened to him but set out for Grint's house alone. Near the Square she spotted the Town Guard and quickly hid in the burnt-out shell of an old building. She waited until the Guard had passed by and it was clear again before leaving the shelter. Nervously she checked she had the moon moss. Yes, there it was. And then quite suddenly it struck her how odd it was that her mother had asked for *fresh* moon moss. It was more potent dry. Why had her mother asked for this...? A sense of unease began to seep through her bones.

Something was not right.

A pale light coming from Grint's windows lit up the old clock tower in the Square but all the surrounding buildings were dark.

The front door was ajar. There were voices coming from inside; they sounded angry and urgent. Crystal crept forward to listen.

'You fool!' Grint was saying. 'I didn't want her hurt! Just kept out of the way a little longer. I need time with Effie – something's wrong with her. For some reason she was remembering things...'

'The skweener was only to try and scare Crystal a little,' Raek said. 'She's too cocky. Too—'

'Oh, my precious skweener! Where is it now? And where is *she*? You stupid idiot! Go back and find her! Effie will never work for me if I don't have her daughter to bargain with. I need them both.'

'Sorry, I...'

'Did you actually see her fall?' Grint asked.

'Er... I think I heard her,' Raek said.

Crystal pushed the door open and went in.

'You!' They spoke at the same time.

Raek stumbled backwards, eyes wide. 'But – you can't be!'

A nerve twitched in Grint's cheek but he looked at her calmly. 'Crystal. You're here: we were worried. Did you get the moon moss?'

Crystal nodded. She wondered if they could see her knees knocking. She held her hands together tightly to try and hide their trembling. She hoped she didn't look as sick as she felt.

'I was worried when you took so long. Raek shouldn't have left you. How would I ever tell your mother I'd let anything bad happen to you?'

'No. I'm fine,' Crystal said. 'How is Mum?'

'The same,' Grint said. 'You'd better come and see her.' As he went past Raek he knocked into him so Raek was thrown against the wall. 'Sorry!' Grint said with a smile.

Crystal followed.

Grint stood back while Crystal placed the moon moss on her mother's forehead, put more into her slack hands and some round her throat like a necklace. 'There, there,' she said. 'That will help you, Mum.'

'She was nervous and jumpy tonight. Not at all her usual self.' Grint looked at Crystal enquiringly. 'Your sly-ugg told Raek everything, you know, before he left. What has Effie been doing?'

'I don't know what you mean,' Crystal said. If the

sly-ugg *had* told him everything, why was he asking her? He was lying. He didn't know anything. 'Mum's probably just a bit off colour.'

She looked up and was shocked to find Morton Grint very close, staring at her, as if he were trying to see inside her head. She smiled as lightly as she could. 'I must keep an eye on her,' she added.

'We must *both* keep an eye on her,' Grint said.

Effie suddenly stirred. Her eyes flew open. 'What happened?'

'Mum! Thank goodness!' Crystal exclaimed. 'I knew we shouldn't have come tonight only—'

'Only Effie is not allowed to miss her sessions with Morton Grint,' Grint reminded her. 'Is she?'

Next day Crystal left Effie sitting by the window stroking Icicle's black fur, and forced herself to go up into the ghostly space above their apartment. She had to find that egg-shaped thing from the lake.

There were seven floors of abandoned apartments upstairs; so many rooms, all empty. The furniture had been stolen and used as firewood long ago. Her footsteps echoed loudly on the dusty floor and seemed to follow her around. She kept looking over her shoulder, thinking she wasn't alone.

There were loads of empty buildings and derelict factories in Town. Giant chimneystacks, blocks of flats, warehouses with a hundred glass-less windows through which the rain dripped. Some of the rooms in the office buildings had machines wired into the walls but those had stopped working at whatever they did long ago. Stella had told her that once the Town had been filled with hundreds of thousands of people. They'd had *electricity* that made the machines work. Then there was the war.

After the war, Grint.

No one knew where Grint came from, or how he arrived, but he took over the Town with no resistance from the Towners. As if he were used to doing that sort of thing. He had the Wall reinforced so people couldn't get in or out. He made rules and laws. He organized the mining of precious metals that they could exchange for food with outsiders. The Town became secure and able to sustain itself again.

Crystal didn't go into every apartment upstairs. The dust on the floor had not been disturbed for years. She was sure her mother had not come here to hide the mystery object.

She clattered down the stairway and let herself into the flat. The first thing she saw was her mum stroking the little black cat. The word *witch* sprang into her head, she couldn't help it. Her mother's hair was stringy; she was muttering to herself, and the kitten was gazing at her from her lap. *Witch.*

'Mum!' She tipped the cat off her mother's lap. 'What did Grint do to you last night? Yesterday you were so, so wonderful! So different...' She almost said, 'So much *nicer*!' and stopped herself. But she felt cheated, as if she'd glimpsed her real mum, and then had her snatched away.

'I don't know what you mean.'

'I know. Neither do I... Listen, it's Saturday,' she went on. 'Food store day. There might be some green vege-tables. You'll enjoy that, won't you?'

Effie shrugged.

'Oh, come on, Mum, even the sly-ugg likes to get out!' she added, sweeping it into the carry-box. 'Let's go.'

They went to the food store once or twice a week. Each person got a certain amount of food depending on their age and what job they did. If you had money you could buy extra rations. A little of the food was grown in Town, but most was tinned and left over from before the war. If it weren't for the medicines Effie made, there would be no extras such as Minty Moments for Crystal.

They stood in the long queue with their tickets ready.

'Hello, Effie.'

'Hi, Stella,' Crystal said. 'Mum, say hello to Stella!'

'Stella?' Effie looked surprised, then cool. 'Stella. How is your father's cousin? How is Annie Scott?' she asked.

Stella's smile slipped from her face. 'Haven't you heard?'

'What?'

'She's dead.'

'Oh, no! Dead? I'm so sorry, Stella!' Crystal said.

'Dead? Oh dear. Oh dear, but I gave her— I must sit down,' Effie said. She sat on one of the hard metal chairs that lined the hall and looked worriedly round the room. She began jiggling the sly-ugg's carry-box on her knee as if it were the kitten.

'Oh dear, I thought Effie'd have known. I'm sure it wasn't her fault – I mean, of course it wasn't.' Stella lowered her voice. 'I didn't know Annie Scott very well.'

'Nor did I. But I *am* sorry,' Crystal said.

'I don't suppose you've heard, you manage to miss most important things, Crystal, but Grint, Bless and Praise his

Name, is really cracking down on witchcraft. Anything can be called sorcery, Crystal, anything, so do take care...'

Crystal nodded.

'You know that somehow Grint found out all about Fred Furkin trying to go over the Wall,' Stella went on. 'He's been arrested. What would Mr Furkin want to do that for? There are only swamps and deserts and mines out there. Isn't Grint amazing? He knows everything, doesn't he?'

Crystal shrugged. She couldn't concentrate. She glanced round at the queues of people shuffling up to the counter. Were they staring at Effie? Did they think she was a witch? Her mum was ill, that was all. It wasn't *her* fault about Annie Scott. She'd developed mysterious lumps on her arms and neck. No one could have cured her. There, those old biddies were staring at Effie and whispering about her, she could tell. Why didn't they leave her alone?

'But I'm sure you've nothing to worry about, Crystal,' Stella continued.

Which only made Crystal more worried.

'We don't blame Effie,' Stella went on, watching Crystal closely. 'For Annie, I mean.'

'Mum tried to help her,' Crystal said.

'Of course she did. The trouble is, everyone's talking about it, I'm afraid. I thought you should know,' she added with a sympathetic smile.

'No one told us.' Crystal swallowed with difficulty; felt a tightening in her insides. Had her mum made some awful mistake? Was she losing her touch? 'I did hear someone had seen a skweener in Town,' Crystal said quickly, changing the subject.

'A skweener?' Stella shivered. 'No! Really? Right here in Town? I think I'd die if I saw one. They are so scary!'

You have no idea just *how* scary, Crystal thought with a shudder.

Effie and Crystal walked slowly back from the food store with their bags of provisions. Crystal tried to chat brightly, but it was so hard. She was fretting over what Stella had said. And she wished her mother wasn't plodding along so heavily beside her looking distracted and... weird.

They were passing an area of scrub, when Effie stopped suddenly. She pointed at a sapling by the wall. 'Look! Oh look, Crystal, a dear little *Spindle tree*! I don't remember ever having seen one here before!'

'How do you know its name, then?'

Effie looked dazed. She blinked and shook her head. 'I don't know.'

'Maybe,' Crystal whispered, pressing the meshed side of the carry-box against her skirt so the sly-ugg couldn't hear, 'maybe the place we came from, the place we used to live, had Spindle trees?'

Effie shook her head. 'Don't ask me. I remember nothing. Nothing at all.'

'If you could remember where we came from, Mum,' Crystal went on quietly, 'we could go back there. The other day you said—'

'How can I remember something when there's nothing there?' Effie shrugged. 'It's empty, empty... But... there's specks floating and sometimes I almost grasp one . . . Like a—'

'What?'

Effie squeezed Crystal's arm. 'Like a snowflake.' She straightened up; her eyes gleamed with a sudden burst of light. 'Just the thought of it! I feel so much more me. *Snowflake!* Come on. Come!'

They walked home quickly.

Crystal put the sly-ugg's carry-box down on the table and swivelled it round to face the wall. She pretended to forget to open it. The sly-ugg could push the lever that held the side closed, but it would take a few minutes – precious minutes she would have unobserved with her mother.

Effie was pulling her bed out from against the wall. She lifted up the torn lino beneath it to reveal wooden planks.

'Mum?'

'Shh!' Effie prised out a strip of wood and took something out from the cavity below. Crystal almost stopped breathing. It must be that thing from Lop Lake. At last!

But it wasn't.

'It's a picture,' Effie said. 'It's for you!'

It was a tiny, framed painting of snow-covered hills. A minuscule man, woman and girl tramped up towards a high peak. Everything was covered in white.

'Touch it,' said Effie.

Crystal touched it. The white surface depicting snow was cold to touch. And it was raised; she could feel it with her fingertips.

'It's been carved out of spindle wood,' her mother said. 'I put it away for safekeeping and forgot . . . It's for you.

He'd only just made it. A present.'

'Who made it?'

'It was... He was... Sorry, Crystal, I don't remember.'

'Never mind.'

Crystal had never seen real snow. It was never cold enough for the lake to freeze or for snow to fall, though she'd heard about it. There were distant places where it snowed.

'So that is snow. It's so beautiful!' Crystal said. 'It's wonderful. I feel, I feel...' She gazed into the picture. 'I feel I know that place. Is it where we were before?'

'Is it? I don't know. Mountains. Hills. Everything covered in white. Snowflakes as big as leaves. A sky so blue and a sun so big and yellow... There's never a sun like that here! Never a sapphire sky. Never anything glinting and sparkling...'

She squeezed Crystal's hands in hers and smiled.

'Oh, Mum!' Crystal had never seen her look so beautiful and happy. 'It must be where we were before we came here—' She spotted a movement; the sly-ugg had oozed into the room and was listening to them with great attention. 'I think it's where we came from,' Crystal said quietly. 'It must be beyond the Wall. We've got to get back there, Mum. We have to!'

Effie sighed loudly. She sank down on her bed. As quickly as her interest and energy had flared up, they'd died again.

'We'll never get out. Nothing is worth bothering about. We are lost, Crystal. Lost.'

8
Greenwood is Low

Questrid had searched his room again. The acorn holder was definitely missing. It *had* to be what Greenwood had thrown into the lake. He was determined to try and talk to him about it as soon as he could.

Next day he was in the kitchen helping Oriole prepare lunch, when a redwing flew in through the window and landed on the back of a chair beside him. A tiny roll of paper was tied around its left leg.

'It's from Greenwood,' Questrid said, reading the message. 'He says thank you for lunch and don't worry about him. He wants to be left alone. I get the feeling he's a bit low.'

That was a nuisance. He was determined to try and talk to him about it as soon as he could, but he didn't want to admit to Greenwood that he'd spied on him. It was very difficult. But then everything about Greenwood was rather difficult. He was calm and kind and solid, and yet Questrid got the feeling he was rather sad. When all the family was together Greenwood was the first to leave a meal, the last to stop work. He was a shadowy splinter of a person.

Questrid turned the slip of paper over and over in his hands. Everyone in the house used the birds to send messages to each other as a matter of course. A small slip of paper, a few tiny letters...

Questrid had not shown anyone the acorn holder except Copper. He'd wanted it to be absolutely perfect before he'd shown it off. Had Greenwood perhaps found it and worked out that it was hollow? Had Greenwood in fact been using it to *send* a message, like in an empty bottle, and not, as Questrid had first thought, been throwing the acorn away?

But then where had the message been going?

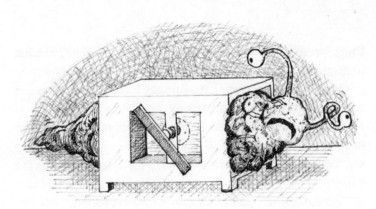

9

Spying on the Spy

The next day, Effie and Crystal had a surprise visit from one of the Town Guard. He brought a summons. Effie had to go to see Grint again that evening.

But why again so soon? Crystal wondered. Was it because Annie Scott had died? Or was it because of her mother's recent odd behaviour? Or was Raek going to try to scare her again?

Crystal had relived that awful flight from the skweener over and over. How could Raek have done that to her? Raek was more hateful than she'd ever imagined he could be. And now because of him the poor animal had died a dreadful death. She would hear the sound of its cries and the thrashing noises in the mud forever and ever.

She must be careful, really careful.

* * *

Raek opened the door for them. He didn't mention what had happened on their last visit. He looked narrowly at Crystal and then snatched the sly-ugg's carry-box from her and set it down on a marble sideboard.

'Put your umbrellas in there,' he said. 'Don't let them drip on the floor. Grint, Bless and Praise his Name, will see you straightaway. It's wet so *you*'d better sit in the waiting room,' he told Crystal. 'Come on, Effie.'

'Why does he want her again?' Crystal asked.

Raek assumed a look of disgust. 'She was no use last visit, was she?' he said bitterly. 'She was ill. Grint, Bless and Praise his Name, wants Effie tonight. Effie must do as he says!'

The small waiting room where Crystal sat was bare except for a line of benches around the walls. No one else was waiting to see Grint. Crystal sat sucking a sweet and staring at a door in the corner. She had never really noticed that door before.

The house was silent. Crystal got up and tried the door. It wasn't locked. It opened onto a long corridor. The walls were close; the floor was made of uneven stone slabs. At the end was a small green metal door.

Crystal went back to the waiting room and sat down. She was shaking. Could she go out that way? Out into the space behind the House and perhaps spy on Grint? Ever since she had found her mother lying on that divan and not in the re-ceiving room, she had been suspicious. Where did Grint take her mother when Crystal left? What did he do to her?

Of course the green door could be locked, but... it might not be.

She got up swiftly, went down the corridor and tried the green door at the end. It opened. Two seconds later she was outside, behind Grint's house in a high-walled garden.

The rain had almost stopped, but anyway Crystal loved the rain. She liked to feel a thin veil of it covering her bare skin; she loved the damp earthy smell rain released from the ground. She loved getting wet.

She ran straight to a group of tall thin trees and stood there looking at the House. This was dangerous! She could hardly get her breath, as if she were wearing a too-tight belt. She'd be in terrible, *awful* trouble if she were caught ...

There were two dimly lit windows on the ground floor of the House. One, she was sure, would be where her mum was. Crystal laid her hand against the slender tree; it exuded a scent – a sort of clean greenness, which made her feel braver.

She scampered over a patch of soil and tufts of grass; the ground was rough with shards of pointed steel, broken pipes and rocks. She stopped beside one of these windows and peeped inside.

It was a laboratory. The walls were lined with shelves of glass tubes and beakers, pots, bottles of powders and strange instruments. On the long metal table in the centre of the room was an open-ended steel box with large screws jutting out on either side.

Raek came in. He didn't glance towards the window and anyway Crystal knew how hard it was to see out into the dark, but she made sure she didn't get too close. He put the carry-box – *their* carry-box with *their* sly-ugg in it –

down on the table and lifted the sly-ugg out with gloved hands. It was droopy and limp.

The window was open and Crystal could hear clearly.

'What can I squeeze out of you tonight, my slimy, slithery, squelchy spy, eh?' Raek said. He got down so low, so close, that mucus from the sly-ugg stuck to his hair and slimed on his cheek. 'Secrets? Got lots of secrets for me, eh? Lovely, lovely secrets?'

The sly-ugg's eyeballs rolled backwards and forwards on the end of their stalks. It hunched itself up as it tried to slither away, but Raek held it tight.

'Oh no, we don't! No escape for you! In we go, you foul slime-ball!'

Raek squashed the sly-ugg into the metal box. Its head stuck out at one end, tail at the other. Its stalk-eyes thrashed around furiously as it bucked and fought; but it was trapped. Raek tightened the screws, turning them slowly until the sly-ugg's head began to bulge like a balloon.

Suddenly there was an awful scream. Crystal jumped. Goose bumps broke out all over her skin. She stared at the sly-ugg, at its open mouth...

The sly-ugg! The sly-ugg was screaming!

Raek was turning the screws and squashing it harder and harder. It eye-stalks flailed about, twisting and knotting up. It writhed and wriggled like a worm on the end of a line.

Crystal felt weak and sick.

Then, quite suddenly, the sly-ugg went still. Its flesh began to glow a brilliant white, as if it were hot. The light that poured from it began to form a beam and the beam of white light condensed and formed a circle on the wall opposite.

'Aha!' Raek roared. 'Here we go!'

He stood back and watched the white circle where an image was gradually appearing... It gave Crystal a jolt. The sly-ugg had recorded everything it had seen at their apartment inside its head and now here it all was, replayed! Everything they'd said and done in front of the sly-ugg had been captured. She had known it was a spy, but still, it was awful to see how good a spy it was!

And if that was what Raek did to the sly-ugg, what was Grint doing to her mother?

Raek squeezed the screws a little tighter.

'Now, slug-bug spy,' Raek said. 'I didn't get as much out of you last time as I think I could have. We have to go back to that smoky day, that special day when Effie got so lively, when she began to *remember*. When she collapsed! You didn't tell me everything. I know there's more. You're hiding something, little sluggy, and you know you mustn't hide things from me. What happened? Something, something... We need to see what she got up to...'

The white circle on the wall became cloudy. Grey swirls of smoke drifted across. There was a noise like thunder, which was the sound of coal slithering out of the coal bucket onto the fire and then the whoosh of water sizzling and steaming. The sly-ugg was replaying the moment when Crystal had tried to outwit it; the time her mum had gone alone to the lake. Raek waved his hands around as if he could actually waft the smoke on the wall away.

'...Can't see a thing! You should have moved faster. You should have recorded everything! Mindless mollusc! Spineless slug! You're no use at all!'

Crystal couldn't watch any more. She was horrified to see what the sly-ugg's spying could do, though she felt sorry for it at the same time. And somehow, *somehow*, it had not seen her mother bring back the thing from the lake. Thank goodness for that!

She edged nervously along to the next window, briefly wondering how long she'd been outside. The rain was starting up again. She was getting wetter but she doubted Raek would notice that. She just had to have a look in the next window. It wasn't the receiving room because that was at the front of the House. If her idea was right, and Grint took Effie somewhere else, this might be the place.

She *was* right. Her mother was there.

Grint too.

There were only two chairs and a table, otherwise the room was bare. And cold. She knew it was cold because both Grint and her mother wore furs: fur cloaks, wraps and hats. Crystal had never seen anything like these skins before. Perhaps they came from some animal beyond the Wall? But why was the room cold? Why—?

Grint suddenly strode towards the window with his arms outstretched. Crystal choked back a terrified scream; he'd seen her!

'Rain's getting in,' he muttered and slammed the wooden shutters shut with a crash.

Crystal leaned against the wall panting, heart thumping. What was going on?

She jumped at a small noise close by. Was someone there? She was so nervous everything made her jump. Her heart thudded fast and painfully against her ribs. She had to get back before Raek found she was missing. She couldn't skirt the garden and go back through the shelter of the trees; she hadn't time. As she ran alongside the house and the crumbling outbuildings, she tripped on something poking up and crashed against a shed door with a horrible metallic clang.

She froze where she landed, crouching on the ground, terribly afraid. She held her breath, hoping that no one had heard.

All was quiet, no doors opening or angry shouts. Then in the silence she heard something, some sort of animal right there, in the shed. She shot away from the door, but the creature, whatever it was, seemed to be locked in. It whimpered softly and whined. Then it sniffed wetly at the crack beneath the door. A dog perhaps? A Minty Moment had fallen from her pocket and was lying by the door. Suddenly a long tongue slipped out from the inky blackness below the door, caught the sweet and hooked it inside.

The creature cried out suddenly, slamming itself against the door with a thundering clatter. The door groaned under its weight and the hinges creaked.

It wasn't a dog.

Crystal ran.

10
The Missing Page

Questrid set off for the library, a room near the very top of Spindle House.

He rarely went there. Firstly, he wasn't very keen on books and reading, and secondly, he didn't like the swaying of the branches and the creaking of the timber, both of which got more violent and louder the higher up you went.

He was looking for information about the Glass Hills and the circular lake. He knew Greenwood's sudden strange behaviour was linked to what had happened there.

Questrid took down the books that contained maps and plans of the Marble Mountains. The tallest peak in the mountains was called the Rock and his mother lived there. The Glass Hills were part of that pointed craggy chain. He found them clearly marked but not the lake. He couldn't find the lake on any of the maps. Then he tried histories. Fishing. Boating. No book mentioned the circular lake inside the Glass Hills. It was well and truly hidden.

He was about to give up when he spotted an old, battered book of Marble Mountain folklore. He flicked through the pages, stopping suddenly at *The Gateway in the Frozen Lake*.

The story was about Pol Lake, which was as round as a plate, as smooth as a mirror, and hidden behind tall glass-like mountains. The lake remained frozen always. Questrid's pulse began to race as he read:

> ...until one year, without warning, the ice will begin to melt. A perfect circle of water will appear in the lake's very centre as the ice shrinks. The water will be of the clearest turquoise blue. It is The Gateway to the World Below. It will not be open for long and it may close behind whoever dares to risk the journey but...

Questrid turned to the next page, but there was no more of the tale, the pages had been torn out.

11

The Ticket to Freedom

'The tickets for the mines trip have come,' Stella told Crystal as they walked back from school a few days later. 'Remember? I told you Dad won them in a raffle.'

'I don't remember.'

'Oh, I did tell you!' Stella said. 'You never remember anything – I don't think you even listen! But, anyway, it doesn't matter because we're *not* going. I'm so disappointed.' She paused as if she were waiting for Crystal to say something. When Crystal didn't speak, she started again. 'It was just Mum and me who *were* going, but Mum thinks it will be too scary. She says there's rockgoyles and skweeners and outsiders who might attack... Of course, I'm not scared, but— And now the tickets will be *wasted*.'

It was the words *Mum and me* that gave Crystal the idea. Why didn't she go with *her* mum? This was their chance to escape! Crystal squeezed Stella's arm. 'Stella!'

'Yes?'

'Could *we* have them? My mum and I? Because you know Mum hasn't been very well and the trip would do her good, I'm sure it would. Something different. Oh, could we?'

She tried not to let the desperation she felt creep into her voice.

'What? Of course you can. What a good idea!' Stella said straightaway. 'We don't want them now... Would Effie really want to see the mines?'

'Maybe not – but I'd like to see them. I mean, you know how I think I'll end up there one day! Better check them out first, eh? But seriously, to be on the other side of the Wall would be such a treat for us both.'

Stella smiled. 'I think it's a brilliant idea,' she said. 'I'm so glad you thought of it!'

They had four days before the trip. Then three. Two. One day to go and they'd be out of this grey city! Crystal wanted to do something to prepare, but she knew she mustn't. It was important she behaved completely normally in front of the sly-ugg and their neighbours. No one must know their plans. Still, despite her efforts, the sly-ugg began to watch her very carefully.

Ever since Crystal had seen what Raek did to it, she'd felt differently about the sly-ugg. It seemed it spied without trying, by accident almost, and then was tortured into revealing what it had recorded. She had started to feed it flower petals and strips of carrot, as much loffseed as it

64

could eat. She had even once stroked its head and it had responded by nudging against her hand, like the cat.

But it was still Grint's spy and she had to keep their plans secret.

After the last visit to Morton Grint, her mother attacked her woodcarving with new energy. It made Crystal's heart hurt to watch her; the way she cut into the wood as if she were in search of something, as if she knew that deep inside the block of oak there was something hidden that she had lost.

A knock at the door made her jump. *Stella!* It had to be Stella and she was going to change her mind and want the tickets back and they'd never escape. I won't answer the door, she thought. I won't.

The knocking grew louder and more insistent until her mum put down her sculpting tools and cried: 'Open the door, Crystal!'

It was Raek. He peered over Crystal's shoulder into the room. 'What's Effie doing? Not making love potions, I hope.'

Crystal was almost too surprised to speak. Then she was scared. Did Raek know about the tickets? She swallowed. 'No. Mum's fine.' She stood back a little so that he could see her mum stroking the cat. The sly-ugg saw Raek and pulled in its eye-stalks as if it had been burned.

'She looks odd,' Raek said. 'A bit deranged.'

'No, she's fine. Thank you.' Crystal pushed the door shut a little.

Raek's face was very red and shiny, as if it had been scrubbed with a hard bristly brush. 'Are *you* OK?' Crystal added.

Raek touched his cheek. 'How dare you ask me something so personal!' he snapped. 'Insolent girl! I came to tell you that Grint, Bless and Praise his Name, requires Effie to make an extra visit this evening. Same time as usual.'

'Again? Not again! Why? We've been twice—'

'Oh now, I think you know the reason. She has been seen behaving strangely. You've only to look at her... There's talk of witchcraft again.'

'Mum's busy tonight. She has a lady coming to get some ointment for her rash.'

'Then the lady will have to cancel.'

'Maybe you'd like some of it instead?' Crystal asked, staring pointedly at Raek's sore cheeks.

He frowned. 'Take care,' he snapped. 'Take care. Look at her with that black cat on her knee! You should watch out, Crystal. Some people in the Town would like to see an end to your mother's potions. An end to her, too!'

Crystal gasped and tried to push the door shut but Raek stuck his foot in the way.

'Can't get rid of me that easily! You should respect me, Crystal; I've told you before. I'm like you. I was an outsider too once. I might be able to help you.'

'I don't want your help. Go away!'

'You'll be sorry, Crystal, I'm warning you.'

He took his foot out of the way and sauntered down the path. 'Until this evening... with the sly-ugg!'

Crystal leaned against the closed door, holding her hand over her racing heart. She looked over at her mum; she had pushed the cat away and was hugging the lump of wood as if it were a long-lost friend.

It was warm but raining again, and Raek put Crystal in the waiting room while her mother was seeing Grint. Crystal was glad; ever since Raek had visited she'd been hoping for this: now she could sneak out again and spy. She had to. This would be her very last chance to see what Grint got up to in that cold room, because tomorrow they'd be gone.

Crystal sat in an old wooden chair waiting for Raek's hard clacking footsteps to die away. The chair was a new addition to the waiting room; it seemed to pulse and tremble beneath her as if it were just about to take off. When they were free of the Town they'd have wooden furniture too. No more metal and stone, but lots of wood. Just sitting in it made her feel stronger.

When it was quiet, she slipped through the door again, down the corridor and out into the garden. She pulled up her hood to keep the rain off her hair and tucked up her long skirt so it wouldn't get muddy.

The shutters were open, so she could see right into the room where Grint and her mother were. The windows were slightly cloudy. Crystal laid her fingertips on the glass; the panes were frosted on the inside.

Grint and Effie were both wrapped in furs and sitting at either end of the iron table. On the table stood a strange, rather beautiful object. It appeared to be made of pearly glass and was about two feet high. It consisted of a central pole carved with faces and peculiar creatures. A slender tube shaped like a telescope passed through it at a right angle near the top. Strange shapes dangled from the crosspiece. Crystal had no idea what it could be.

She was alarmed at the way her mum looked. Effie's fair skin was snow white, the shadows beneath her eyes plum purple. Despite the furs she still appeared cold. And she looked even more blank than usual, as if she wasn't there at all, as if her eyes and ears weren't really working. She looked like a paper cutout of herself. A nerve twitching in her temple was the only sign of any life.

'Effie! Come on!' Grint said. 'Read it! Tell me what it says!'

'Icicle,' said Effie, softly, resting her fingertips against the glass crosspiece. 'It's beautiful. Cold.'

Icicle? Like the kitten? Cold? Was it made of ice then, not glass? That would explain the icy room, Crystal thought.

'Don't touch it too much,' Grint said. 'I don't want it damaged. We'll never get another one of these, Effie, will we? Because we can't go back up there, back to the Marble Mountains, can we?' Effie flinched, as if something he'd said had finally got through to her. '*Marble Mountains?* Do you remember? No, you don't, not really and it's just as well ... Come on, now. I want a *fortune*. Make it play a fortune, Effie. *Effie!* You know you can do better than this. You're not really trying. I've been very fair up to now, very fair. Just remember little Crystal,' he went on. 'You wouldn't want any harm to come to her, would you?'

Effie jumped as if a small electric pulse had jolted her. 'Don't hurt Crystal!'

'There we go. A reaction. Good. Now, Effie, just imagine Crystal out there in the mines—'

'No!'

'. . . out in the mines, knee-deep in mud, freezing cold and dressed in rags. Snakes slithering round her ankles. Rockgoyles as her bosses! She'd be so scared, Effie. Rockgoyles are evil creatures. And she'd be lonely. Miserable. She wouldn't die – at least not straightaway – but she'd be unhappy and get sick, she'd be hungry and—'

'Be quiet! Don't say those things!'

'I'll be quiet when you start using this!' He pointed to the strange ice thing. 'Tell me what it's saying!'

Suddenly the dangling objects on the icicle began to jiggle and bounce. They produced a faint tinkling melody.

'Is it a fortune?' Grint asked. 'Come on, Effie! You'll be in trouble if you don't look. I swear you will! I'll see that daughter of yours off to the mines if you don't do this. Or there's still a skweener to scare her with. I'll—'

With what seemed an enormous effort, Effie leaned over the table and put her eye against the end of the crosspiece.

'Is it a pastune or a fortune? *Look!*' Grint raked his hands through his long hair. 'Can't you make a picture come? I'm sure you could if you tried. Those damned ice pixies didn't have any problems using these things. I saw them doing it.'

'Pixies?' Effie sat up.

'Oh, it doesn't matter. I was just remembering, back up there, on top, the pixie creatures that made these things.

They could see so much, backwards and forwards in time. You're not trying!'

With a sigh, Effie slowly leaned over the table so she could see into the horizontal tube again. A tear dribbled down her cheek.

'This is a pastune,' she said quietly. 'I can see Molly Webber in her garden. She's planting carrots.'

'For crying out loud!' Grint roared. 'Carrots! Molly Webber! I'm not interested in gardening. I want to know what important things are *going* to happen!'

There was silence in the room for a whole minute then another tune rippled across the ice sculpture.

'Fortune. John Carter,' Effie said. Her voice was flat and expressionless and Crystal realized that her mother had no idea what she was saying because she would never give out information about Stella's father like this. 'He's plotting against Morton Grint. He wants to be the new leader. He is going to challenge Morton Grint. He has not forgiven Morton Grint for putting him down in front of the others. He plans to surprise him at the next meeting.' She spoke as if what she said had no meaning and was of no importance.

Grint, however, leaped up and clapped his hands.

'Ha! I shall be ready! Well done! It's good. It's good. What else?'

'A pastune,' Effie said, staring into the ice tube. 'Mrs Wilkins made a love potion for Mary Smith to make Jim Collett fall in love with her—'

'Love potions are forbidden! That's witchcraft. I'll stop that. She will be punished.' He wrote down the names quickly in a small notebook.

70

Effie's flat voice went on. 'This is a fortune: there will be more trouble from the Barnaby Andrews family. They don't understand how you found out he was going to rebel... They blame Sam Smith. There is unrest. Trouble is coming to Morton Grint.' Her voice was getting weaker and weaker.

'Good, good! As long as we're forewarned we can win. This is no trouble at all for me. More. Come on, give me more. Crystal's happiness is at stake here, Effie. Remember that!'

'Another fortune. I can see... something going on at the Wall, at the West Gate. I don't understand what it is, Morton Grint... It looks like... I can see...' Effie's voice trembled and shook, as if what she was seeing was too awful or incomprehensible to describe.

There was a sudden clap of thunder overhead and Crystal jumped. Every nerve in her body was jangling and her brain was spinning. She moved away from the window.

She hadn't understood everything, but enough to know that the 'icicle' on the table was what was draining her mother's strength and taking away her memory. And this was why Grint appeared so clever, always one step ahead of the Towers: he used Effie and the 'icicle' as a sort of oracle, to see into the future.

A flash of lightning was followed by rain suddenly splintering down around her. Crystal ran towards the green door, but passing the shed she heard an awful moan and stopped. The creature! Perhaps it was scared of the storm? Lonely? Hungry? Forgetting about the danger she was in, she searched her pockets. She found a sweet, half an apple and a bunch of herbs. Kneeling down quickly at the door, she whispered, 'Hello?'

There was a snuffling and whining in reply from behind the door.

'Here's some food,' she said. 'I've got you some food.' She didn't suppose that the creature, whatever it was, could understand, but she sympathized with it being locked up. She put the food close to the bottom of the door, and then, fearing for her fingers, pushed it nearer with a stick.

There was silence, total stillness on the other side, and then the long tongue slipped out and hooked first the apple in, then the rest.

'Sorry I haven't more,' she whispered. 'Sorry you're in there, whatever you are. I know what it's like being a prisoner.'

12

Crystal Reaches the West Gate

The day of the trip arrived.

Crystal stoked Icicle's silky ears. 'Goodbye, kitty!' The kitten mewed sadly, as if he knew what was happening. 'Sorry, puss,' she whispered into his black fur. 'I've left a note with Mrs Babbage to feed you. I know she loves you and she's always wanted a cat. You'll be happy with her. I wish we could take you, but pets aren't allowed through the gates and anyway, Icicle, we don't know what it will be like out there. We may be making a terrible mistake... Best you stay here.' A shiver rippled through her. Too late for worrying now. 'Are you ready, Mum?'

Effie was sitting by the window with her half-carved piece of wood on the round table in front of her. 'I don't want to go anywhere. I've told you, Crystal, I want to stay here.'

'I know, I know, but... Listen, Mum, look at me. Do you remember what you and Grint talked about last night?'

'No. I never remember, you know I don't.'

'You don't remember being cold? An icy room? A sculpture made of ice that you looked through?'

Panic flashed across Effie's face as if she did remember and Crystal squeezed her hand encouragingly. 'You do? I see you do!'

'No,' her mum said. And the spark of light in her eyes vanished. She shrugged. 'I just want to stay here, Crystal, please.'

Now Crystal was more certain than ever that she was right to get her away from Grint. 'I know, I know, but the trip will do you good. It will be fun. We'll have a good day, Mum, I know we will.'

She put her mother's cloak round her shoulders and urged her to stand up. 'There we go. Trust me.' She pushed her gently towards the door. 'Come on, Mum.'

Just as they were about to leave, a sudden high-pitched, urgent whine filled the room. Crystal stood rock still; the hairs on the back of her neck prickled. It was not a noise that could be ignored.

'I forgot the sly-ugg.' She stared at it. She didn't want to take it. But if she left it here it would go on crying and someone would come. She didn't want Raek to torture it again either. She quickly scooped it up in the carry-box. Perhaps she could set it free somewhere? Somewhere beyond the Wall?

'I don't want to do this, Crystal,' her mum said as Crystal closed the door of the apartment. 'It's not a good idea.'

Crystal turned the key and put it under the stone by the step. Her mum was probably right. And now she would never find the egg-shaped object from Lop Lake. Crystal would never know why Effie had briefly changed, but it was too late. The answer to the puzzle of their past had to be beyond the Wall – and that's where they were going.

The tour bus was a covered wagon pulled by four very large horses. It was parked in the Square by the clock tower. The other Towners who had tickets for the trip to the mines were chattering and laughing, excited about their outing. Crystal could barely stop herself from shaking. She kept glancing at Grint's house. If he saw her, would he stop her? Just to be safe, she kept the wagon between her and his house.

Mrs Hopkins, who lived two blocks north of them, was also going. 'Never thought of you and your mum being interested in this sort of trip,' she said. 'To tell you the truth, I don't think I am either. I mean, it's a bit like gloating over the misfortunes of others, isn't it? Seeing the ugly old rockgoyles slaving away and all those folk that have been banished having to live like animals in holes.'

Crystal nodded. 'Yes. No. I mean, well, we got the tickets for free and—'

'I know, you feel you have to, don't you, when everyone else wants to go? I really don't think Effie will enjoy it. But the scenery's nice. I went two years ago. Shame about Annie Scott passing on, wasn't it? Still, with those lumps and bulges and that fever, she was unlikely to recover. Well, I hope you're right about your mum, dear, she doesn't look too good to me.'

'She's fine,' Crystal said. 'She's looking forward to it. Really.' Nothing could be further from the truth. Effie was tense and her fingers constantly snatched at her bag as if she were going to open it but couldn't remember how. Her blue eyes darted backwards and forwards nervously.

'Crystal, Crystal,' she muttered.

'Yes, Mum, what is it?'

'Something. I don't know. I can't think. I wish I could think but my mind, when I try, it's all cloudy and cold.'

'Never mind. It'll be all right soon, I promise.'

'Something. Something's wrong.'

'Shh. Don't worry.'

Crystal sounded so certain but inside she was as worried as her mother. She had no idea what they would find on the other side of the Wall or how they would escape. She just knew she couldn't let such a good opportunity slip by.

The driver glanced at their tickets and punched a hole in them. 'Welcome aboard!'

Crystal's heart was thudding painfully as she and her mum got to their seats. She put the carry-box on her knees. The sly-ugg was quiet, munching on the stack of loffseed she'd put in with it. Once they were outside the Wall, she'd give it to someone, lose it somehow.

Trips to the mines only ran three times a year. Crystal could hardly believe her luck in getting *these* tickets at *this* time. She knew some of the day-trippers were hoping to pick up precious stones or maybe some rare fruit grown outside the Town that the mine chiefs would have for sale. Not her. She just wanted to get out. In thirty minutes, she thought, they would reach the Wall. In thirty-five they would be on the other side. Free. It was all so easy. Why hadn't she done this before? They might have been free years ago! They were going to find their home. The snow! The mountains! Those things must be out there somewhere. She slipped her little painting out from her bag. Snow. She had that clue to the puzzle of her past – if only she'd managed to find the mysterious egg-object before they'd left too, she was certain that was somehow important.

They passed down grey streets, shells of buildings, collapsed towers and empty blocks. Here and there amongst the bricks and fallen steel and concrete, grass was growing. High up on the windowsills and rooftops small patches of flowers and baby trees were sprouting. It made Crystal smile. Perhaps in years to come it would all be green. That would be so much nicer than grey.

'Where are we going?' Effie was looking up and down the streets anxiously. 'Where? Why are you telling me to hush! What is it?'

'Nothing. We're going to see the mines. It's a treat. I told you.'

'The mines? What are the mines, Crystal?'

'Shh. Where they dig up Grint's precious metals,' Crystal said quietly. 'You know.'

'Metal and rock,' her mum said. 'Solid and hard.'

'Yes, that's right.'

'It's bad, Crystal, bad.'

There were four gates in the Wall and each was heavily guarded. The Town Guard would search their papers. Maybe their names were on a wanted list. She could imagine they might be on a list of people not allowed out. Grint might do that. She could feel her heart pounding madly and her hands were sweating. It was hard to breathe. They were getting closer and closer to the West Gate. The Wall loomed up beside them, towering a hundred metres high like a dark red cliff.

The Town Guard was there; the gold buttons on their jackets glinted. There were so many men, row upon row, as if they expected trouble.

Effie suddenly sat up. For the first time she seemed to see her surroundings.

'Where are we?'

'Just coming to the West Gate.'

'You didn't tell me we were coming *here*.'

'I did. Mum, hush, we're going out to see the mines and—'

'We're not! I know we're not.' Effie stood up and overbalanced, falling back onto the seat. People stared. 'Oh, Crystal, no! This is terrible!'

'Sit down, Mum. Please!'

'We shouldn't have come!'

The wagon stopped in the deep cold shadow of the vast Wall. The West Gate was open and everyone was trying to look through it. Crystal glimpsed pale hills stretching away into the distance. She imagined snow-covered mountains and icy rivers. She longed to run there.

Suddenly two groups of the Town Guard detached themselves smoothly from the ranks and surrounded the wagon. In one neat manoeuvre they raised their spiked staffs and pointed them at the vehicle.

'What's the matter?' asked the driver. 'It's only me and the mines tour.' He laughed. 'What's going on?'

'Sorry, mate,' said a guard with a silvery helmet. 'You can't go through. We've had word from John Carter to search the wagon. Everyone out! You've got robbers on board!'

John Carter? Crystal was surprised. That was Stella's father – what had he got to do with robbers?

There were moans and complaints as everyone climbed down and was made to stand in a huddle beside the wagon. Some of the guards kept up the fence of pikestaffs; others climbed onto the cart and began to search it.

Crystal's legs were weak; her knees longed to fold so she could sit down. She could not keep herself from staring out at the free, vast landscape through the big gateway. She just knew there would be clear water there: waterfalls, pools, rivers, oceans. And she was close. So close ...

'I saw this,' Effie whispered to her. 'I remember seeing all this, as if it was in a mirror. It was flat and bare, but I saw it. Why do I always remember too late?'

'What do you remember?' Crystal whispered back.

'The gate, the guards ... I saw them ...'

The other Towners were muttering quietly to each other too. Crystal knew that some were glancing over towards her and her mother as if this delay was something to do with them. It was dreadful to be different. Perhaps they should have dyed their hair for the trip? Perhaps they should have dyed their hair long, long ago. But how could they ever hide their blue eyes?

A tall guard jumped down from the wagon. 'Who was sitting in seats thirteen and fourteen?' he demanded.

Crystal stared at her feet.

'Hang on a minute.' The driver was checking his papers. He read out from his list: 'Seats thirteen and fourteen, was it? Effie and Crystal Waters, that was.'

The other travellers turned and stared at them. Then began to shift back, putting as much distance between the Waters and themselves as they could.

The guard held up the sly-ugg's carry-box that Crystal had left under the seat. 'They were trying to smuggle out a sly-ugg,' he said.

'We weren't!' Crystal cried. 'I didn't know you couldn't take it. You know we have to take it with us everywhere, so of course we took it. Anyway, it wanted to come!'

'Sly-uggs do not have wishes or wants. It is highly illegal behaviour. And look here! This is what we were looking for, a gold candlestick belonging to Grint, Bless and Praise his Name. It has his initials on it. John Carter suspected Effie Waters had stolen it and he was right. She was probably going to try and sell it to the mine chiefs.'

'She didn't!' Crystal cried. 'It's not true! I don't know how that got there. It wasn't—'

Suddenly she knew. It was as shocking as being drenched with cold water. She remembered how keen Stella had been to get her on the trip, how delighted she'd been to give up her tickets. She recalled Stella's cold knowing smile.

Stella, surely not you! The Carters, father and daughter, had set them up!

'Arrest them!' the guard cried.

Immediately they were surrounded. Two burly guards grabbed Crystal and held her arms behind her back. Two more took hold of her mother and marched her off to their office. It all happened quickly, so quickly Crystal could hardly believe everything had gone so completely wrong.

'Mum, Mum!' Crystal struggled against the strong hands. But they had already got her mother through the door of the West Gate office and she was out of sight.

'Stop yelling!' the guard said. 'She'll be taken to the prison for questioning. You can see her later.'

'She didn't do anything wrong!' Crystal sobbed. 'It's not fair! We didn't steal anything!'

'Not how it looks to us,' said the guard.

'But it's true! Wha-what about me?' Crystal asked.

'Back home for you,' he said. 'You're a minor so you aren't responsible. Mr Carter has had his eye on that Effie Waters for some time, I understand. Here, take your horrid sly-ugg and get off back to your block.'

'But I want my mum!'

'Do as you're told, go on!'

The other guards began to usher the Towners onto the wagon. They got back on with obvious relief. Once they were safe in their seats they peered down at Crystal as if she were something disgusting, something unclean. The driver gave her a sad little smile as he returned to his place and chivvied the horses to go. The wagon disappeared through the gateway and the great gates slowly closed behind them.

* * *

The black kitten had disappeared, so Crystal sat in the apartment alone. Alone, except for the sly-ugg who had curled up in its carry-box on the table where she had left it. She could see it had shrunk into the corner, as if it were shy or suddenly nervous of her.

'What's up with you?' she asked it crossly, opening its box. 'You've nothing to worry about, you horrid little worm.' The sly-ugg cringed and she regretted her words immediately. 'Sorry.'

She felt leaden. She couldn't move. She looked round at the grey walls and metal furniture. She hated it so much! And she'd really thought this morning that she would never see it again.

Of course her mother had not stolen the candlestick. That weasel, John Carter, had planted it in their seats knowing exactly which ones they would be sitting in. And she had actually thought that because Mr Carter sometimes spoke up against Grint he might have been on their side. But he was no different from the rest. The injustice of it all! What a false friend Stella had turned out to be! The Guard had been expecting them at the West Gate all along...

West Gate.

She tried to think but her brain felt like treacle. Her mother had mentioned the West Gate to Grint. She must have seen it in the icicle thing. A fortune, that's what she'd said. And she'd told Grint about it just as she told Grint everything... and Grint, or Grint and Carter, had fixed for them to be arrested.

They would never escape now.

The sly-ugg slithered warily out of its box and waved its eye-stalks about. It oozed over the table and came and sat close to her.

Crystal moved away. She wanted the kitten; she wanted to stroke his smooth warm fur and have him cuddle under her neck.

The sly-ugg slimed over the table, keeping its eyes focused on Crystal all the time. Crystal watched it, vaguely wondering what it was up to. Then, as if it hadn't noticed the table edge at all, the sly-ugg dropped into the kitten's basket with a damp *plop*.

'That's not *your* bed!' Crystal tipped the sly-ugg out and the kitten's red cushion tumbled out with it.

And something else.

Something egg-shaped.

Crystal knew immediately it was the thing from Lop Lake that her mother had caught.

She picked it up and rolled it around in her fingers, examining it. It was a beautiful green stone acorn in an acorn cup. As she rolled it, the two sections fell apart. For a second she thought it was broken, until she saw the tiny roll of paper inside.

I'm forever waiting for you. Hope never dies. Greenwood. XXX

Crystal's knees gave way and she sat down with a thud.

The sly-ugg had wormed up the table leg and was staring at her. It was smiling, she was sure it was smiling and yet she didn't think they could, that they did. Had

83

the sly-ugg *shown* her where the acorn was? Was that it? Of course, it probably *had* watched her mother when she came back from Lop Lake that day when the smoke had cleared. Of *course* it had seen what Effie had done with the acorn and yet it hadn't revealed anything to Raek – even under torture. She looked at the sly-ugg again. It was definitely, certainly smiling. Had it come over to *their* side? Had she got a friend where she least expected it?

Crystal got up and brought the sly-ugg a few leaves of loffseed. Its eyes gleamed and it gobbled them up with delight. She was sorry now; sorry for all the bad thoughts she'd had about it. She quickly heaped more herbs on the chair for the sly-ugg before picking the acorn up again.

Somehow this was good, this acorn felt *good* – it felt hopeful. Greenwood, whoever he was, was hope. But where was he? How did he exist in Lop Lake? She never for one moment doubted that the acorn and its message were for Effie and her. They were. She knew it.

She quite suddenly wasn't sad any more. She actually felt optimistic and almost happy. It was bizarre.

She turned the slip of paper over and wrote on the back of it. Carefully she put the message back inside the acorn and screwed the two parts tightly together.

She paused at the doorway – the sly-ugg wasn't going to stop her. It wasn't going to cry out. It went on nibbling quietly on the leaves, looking up at her only for a second with a kindly look, before returning to its food.

She was free.

Outside, the sky was overcast and heavy. The trees' shrunken leaves trembled in the wind and the smell of the lake came down to meet her.

She stood at the water's edge, breathing in the magical scent of water; and thinking of her mother, she threw the acorn into Lop Lake with all her force.

13
Questrid's Plan

Snow was falling in the Marble Mountains, large light snowflakes that drifted and clung to everything. As Questrid worked outside in front of the stables, he acquired a thin covering of white, too, like sugar icing.

'What's all that noise, Questrid? What are you doing?' Robin cried, coming out into the yard. 'Silver's barking in sympathy.'

'*Caw, caw,*' the jackdaw on Robin's shoulder cried.

Questrid was kneeling in the snow. 'Oh, nothing,' he said, waving a hammer around.

'When people start hammering and banging,' Robin said, 'and make a lot of noise which they don't normally do, and then call it nothing, it's usually something.'

Questrid grinned. 'Sorry. Secret.'

'You're not up to anything you shouldn't be, are you?' Robin asked, feeding the jackdaw a slice of apple.

'Nothing I shouldn't be doing, I promise.'

'Only we're responsible for you,' Robin went on. 'We don't want anything to happen to you.'

'You can trust me, Robin. I'm making something—'

'Out of *wood*?'

Questrid looked squarely at Robin. 'Yes, wood. If Copper can do it, I can too. I'm just as much part of the Wood tribe as she is.'

'She's not a *natural* with wood and neither are you! That looks like a tabletop! I can't think why you'd want to make a tabletop.'

'*Robin!*'

Robin chuckled. 'OK. I understand you don't want to tell me.' He walked away whistling, and the jackdaw joined in.

Questrid had to admit that his carpentry did look like a tabletop, but it was supposed to be a raft. Working with wood did not come easily to him, and he was using flighty-wood, which was notorious for being difficult. But it was also known to be the best for building things to float. He'd lashed the planks together with thin rope and filled the gaps with glued-up sawdust.

Why did anyone want to do anything with this woody stuff? he thought, extracting a long splinter out of his finger. And why, when my father was from the Wood tribe, am I so much more a Stone person? Come to think of it, from whom do I get my tracking skills? He scratched his head. Ah me! One day I'll invent a stone boat that can follow wave patterns!

At last he was finished. He went to tell Oriole that he would be gone for the afternoon and to get the latest news on Greenwood from her.

'He's still very peculiar,' Oriole said sadly. 'I don't know... He's talked more the last day than he ever did all the years I've been here! It's like something's been unlocked or broken open or something. Mind you, it's all gobbledegook. What *is* wrong with him?'

Questrid shrugged. 'I don't know. Anyway, he'll be fine here with you and Robin looking after him, won't he?' he said.

'Of course he will. You take care!'

Questrid tied the raft and paddles on top of his sledge and set out up the hill, pulling it behind him.

He arrived at Pol Lake a few hours later.

The icy walls rose up steeply around him, trapping the still, fresh air. There was no doubt it was a magical place, but what secrets did it hold? Was there really a gateway to another world as the book said? And what could it have to do with Greenwood's odd behaviour?

He tramped across the ice pulling the sledge over the smooth glassy surface behind him. He was alert to any cracks or warning groans meaning the ice might give way. A couple of metres from the meltwater he stopped. He untied the raft and the makeshift paddles, and left the sledge there. Now he inched forward, pulling the light raft behind him. When the ice was so thin that it creaked and sunk under him, wetting his boots, he stopped. He got gently onto the raft and pushed off from the ice.

After four heaves and arm-aching pushes, Questrid was afloat in the magical pool. He held his paddles and let the raft drift. The only sound was the water lapping gently and the soft sighs of the ice shifting around him.

He paddled right into the centre of the pool and took out a thick wedge of glass from the safety of his backpack. He had fitted a holder round it so he could place it on the surface, just like a large diving mask.

He was kneeling, about to put his face right up to the glass, when a light breeze suddenly stroked his cheeks and he stopped what he was doing.

The sun appeared, startlingly bright as it slipped out from behind the great white billowing clouds.

The water shifted and a bubble blew up and exploded with a pop right in front of him. The raft rocked. He steadied himself. He felt his heart pitter-pattering: he almost laughed.

Ripples flipped and waved and skittered.

Something was coming! He could see something charging up through the depths below like a torpedo. It got closer and closer and then shot out with a splash, soaring straight out and up into the air.

His acorn holder!

It soared through the air, tumbled onto the ice and rolled away, safe from the water's edge. Questrid turned back to where the bubble had exploded. Quickly he laid the glass mask on the water.

He had no idea what to expect but he knew there'd be something.

What he saw was a lake. And a girl.

It was as if he were looking down through the top of an hourglass; the view below narrowed and then spread out again. Far below, there was a small round lake of dirty grey water. Bent and gnarled trees surrounded it. Beside the water stood a girl with white-blonde hair. And she was staring straight up at him.

'Hello!' he yelled. 'Hello! Can you see me?' He thought she had seen him, thought a faint jolt had passed through her, and was so excited that he wobbled the glass. The vision trembled and blurred and disappeared.

By the time the water was calm enough to look through again, the girl had disappeared.

14
Prison

Crystal gazed at the ripples on the lake where the stone acorn had disappeared. I'm going as crazy as Mum, she told herself. As if there could be anyone at the bottom of the lake. As if there is anyone anywhere who can help me.

And yet she had thought for one fleeting moment that she'd seen a face a long way off, peering up at her through the water. But there couldn't have been anyone... Could there?

She trudged back home, less hopeful without the feel of the smooth, cold stone acorn in her hand. She built up the fire in the living room, glad to have the crackle and hiss of the burning coal. What wonderful stuff coal was, she reflected. She knew it was made from ancient dead trees that had got squashed and gone solid. Those trees had captured the sun's strength and now here it was being released as fire. Wood was wonderful stuff.

Seeing her mother's little brown envelopes of powders and herbs drying near the hearth, she threw them on the fire too. No more of that, ever! Any herbs were strictly for the sly-ugg to eat and nothing else.

The sly-ugg was watching her closely.

'Thank you for showing me where the acorn was,' Crystal told it. 'I'd never have found it. I don't know what it means, but it made Mum happy and it made me happy. And listen, Sly-ugg, I know what Raek does and I'm never taking you back there. Ever. I promise. No more squeezing. OK?'

The sly-ugg's eye-stalks danced and a golden glow began to creep over its skin.

'Happy?'

The sly-ugg's mouth curved into a wide smile.

'Aha! I was right. You *can* smile! Well well, if I'd known that before maybe I'd have been nicer to you. Sorry, Sly-ugg.' Crystal looked at the clock. 'We've a long wait. The guards told me I'm not allowed in the prison to see Mum until four o'clock,' she said. 'Now it's just you and me.'

The day dragged by. Crystal tidied the rooms, stared into the fire, talked to the sly-ugg, worried about her mum and wondered about the acorn.

At last it was time for them to go.

'Come on, Sly-ugg!' The sly-ugg obligingly oozed into its carry-box on its own. 'Mum always said we were prisoners,' she told the sly-ugg as she set off towards the prison, 'but I didn't believe her. Or rather I didn't under-stand what she meant. But she was right. Grint trapped us. He's made her forget everything so she can't go home because she doesn't know where it is.'

Nearer the Square there were more people on the streets and she noticed how the Towners avoided looking at her. Mrs Babbage was the only person who spoke to her. 'Don't worry, dear, your mum will be fine. Grint, Bless and Praise his Name, will see sense in the end. And in case you're worrying, I've got the kitten,' she said. 'He seems to have moved in with me!'

'Thanks,' Crystal said.

Mrs Babbage patted her arm, looked around a little nervously, as if she shouldn't be seen talking to her, and hurried off.

'They know about Mum being in prison,' she told the sly-ugg. 'I suppose you're a prisoner too, aren't you?' she added. 'You have to live with us and I bet you don't want to.'

Three girls from her school swung round the corner and almost bumped into her.

'Oh, look at Crystal Waters! Talking to herself like she's barmy!'

'Mad as her mad mother!'

'Are you off to the prison to see her?'

'Now you're not so grand, are you?'

'We always knew you two were bad ones,' the first said again. 'Now it's proven. A thief and a witch!'

'Liar!' Crystal cried. 'We're not!'

'It's all over Town. Your mother's going to be tried as a witch!'

'My mother is not a thief or a witch,' Crystal said

quietly. 'Grint, Bless and Praise his Name, will release her very soon. It's all been a mistake.'

The other girls shrieked with laughter. 'Yeah! Sure!' They strolled away, arms linked, chattering.

'We never liked you anyway!' one of the girls called out over her shoulder. 'Freak!'

Crystal joined the dismal queue of people quietly waiting outside the prison. She leaned back against the gritty walls and stared up at the grey sky. The sly-ugg stared out too. She wondered if it was listening to the Towners around her and if it would remember everything it had heard.

While she waited for the doors to open she crunched her way through two Minty Moments, savouring the strong sharp taste because she knew it might be a long time before she got more.

At last the big iron doors squealed open and the guards guided the visitors in.

The prison block was horrible. It smelled of dirty socks and rancid cheese. Every time the visitors were moved from one room to another, doors clanged shut with nerve-jangling squeals and keys grated as they were turned in locks. Finally Crystal was shown into a vast, echoing hall where the female prisoners sat at small tables dotted around the room. They each wore identical brown dresses. It wasn't difficult to spot her mum's blonde hair amongst all the dark heads, and Crystal ran towards her.

'Mum, Mum! It's so good to see you! I've been so scared!' Crystal hugged her tightly. 'Are you all right?

They haven't hurt you?' She searched her mother's face for a clue to her state of mind.

Effie looked round the room furtively as she patted Crystal's arm. 'I'm all right, darling,' she said. And she did look well, neither crazy nor in a trance. 'My mind's clearing. Now I'm locked in here, *he* can't get me, can he? Something has shifted, come unstuck. I'm beginning to get my mind back. Now I'm away from him and the eye-cycle...'

'Icicle?'

'*Eye-cycle*. E-y-e-c-y-c-l-e,' she spelled out. 'It tells fortunes. It was made by pixicles.'

'Mum, all these *words*! What's a pixicle?'

'Of course, you don't know. Pixicles are very small pixies that lives in the Marble Mountains. They build beautiful ice houses – at night when they put their lights on you can see right through them. They wear soft blue, white and grey clothes and if they stand very still they're so pale they just disappear into the landscape. But when they want you to see them they wear brightly-coloured hats. They are good folk, the pixicles... Grint was using me to see the fortunes and pastunes in the eye-cycle and to give information to him. I don't have the skills the pixicles have, of course, but we're all from the Water tribe and that's why I could read the eye-cycles. Sometimes I foretold important things that must have helped Grint stay in power.'

'I saw you. I spied through the window, but when I told you about it later you didn't remember anything at all.'

'Didn't I? Each time I read the eye-cycle I lost more memory,' she said. 'Each time my brain got cloudier and softer and I got more stupid. I saw a fortune that showed *us* at the West Gate. I must have told Grint! But anyway, Carter set us up. He got Stella to talk about the tickets and pretend they didn't want them. She made sure you took them, didn't she? Then her father made sure we were stopped and arrested by planting that candlestick. Your plan was doomed, Crystal – right from the start.'

Crystal nodded. 'Sorry, Mum. What's Mr Carter got against us anyway?'

'John Carter wants to get rid of me because he suspects that I help Grint predict things. And he's always been suspicious of us. He's as narrow-minded as the rest of the Towners. And I never trusted Stella.'

'I thought she was my friend.'

'Poor thing!'

Crystal didn't want to dwell on Stella. 'I found the acorn, Mum, the one that came from Lop Lake.'

Effie looked puzzled. 'I never had an acorn, did I?'

'You did. You don't remember. I'm sure the acorn sparked off your memory. Remember how happy you were when you found it? No, you don't, but you were. And, you don't know about this, Mum, but the sly-ugg's changed. It's much nicer. *That* started after the acorn came. I'm sure it did, because it didn't tell Raek about you going to the lake and everything. It's all connected. And, Mum, you'll never believe it, but there was a message inside the acorn! It said—'

She stopped. The room had grown quiet and still; everyone was looking towards the door. There stood Raek.

Crystal saw a tiny movement out of the corner of her eye. The sly-ugg, which up until now had been listening closely, was inching under the table out of sight.

The prison guard pointed out Effie, and Raek moved towards her purposefully, weaving around the tables like a thin grey stick. Visitors and prisoners nodded and bowed as he walked past, and then quickly turned away to begin whispering again.

'How kind of you to visit us,' Crystal said. 'I'm sorry we can't offer you tea.'

'Tut, tut, still very rude,' Raek said shaking his head. 'I didn't come for tea, of course. I did warn you, Crystal,' he went on, 'and now your mother is in serious trouble. Stealing. Attempting to take a sly-ugg out of the Town. Lying. She can't escape punishment.'

Effie didn't look at him. She studied the dirty scratched wall and rocked backwards and forwards slowly.

'Did she take that in?' Raek asked Crystal. 'Should I say it louder?'

'She's not deaf, just unwell,' Crystal said quickly. 'I can't make her understand anything. She isn't talking sense.'

Effie picked up the water jug and began pouring water into the glass and back again, in and out, and in and out.

'She likes the sound the water makes,' Crystal explained. 'Sorry.'

'It looked as if she was talking sense a moment ago,' Raek snapped.

'Oh, no, she wasn't,' Crystal said. 'Nothing but rubbish.' Her blue eyes challenged Raek to disagree.

He sighed. 'Well – perhaps it's for the best. If she knew what was going to happen to her... Grint, Bless and Praise his Name, wanted her sentence reduced because of her illness and the help she gives him, but the Elders felt that she should be made an example of and I agree. John Carter is very persuasive. Effie was initially charged with stealing the candlestick, for which the punishment is banishment to the mines. After a meeting, however, the Elders decided that her dabbling in black magic and witchcraft is a much worse offence and will bring a harsher punishment. Her implication in the death of that woman, Annie Scott, was the final straw.'

'Mum never—'

But Raek blanked her out with his hand. 'Silence.'

Crystal stood up. She felt herself trembling and put her hands on the table to steady herself. 'Mum's not well. It isn't fair! It was me—'

'She was well enough to steal. Well enough to concoct magic potions that kill. Well enough to try and put a spell on Grint, Bless and Praise his Name! Oh yes, she tried that all right with her moon moss and lichens, herbs and potions. She will be punished most severely! And,' he added, pointing to the carry-box, 'I'll take that.'

'Oh no, you can't!' Crystal said. 'I mean, Grint, Bless and Praise his What's It, told me that I had to bring *him* the sly-ugg. He was very clear about that. I promised—'

Raek smiled; he knew she was lying.

'Thank you!' He picked up the carry-box. 'It's very light!' He peered through the mesh screen. 'It's empty! Where is the sly-ugg? Where are you hiding it? Give it back!'

'I don't know what you mean,' Crystal said. 'Of course we're not hiding it! We hate it!' But she was thrilled. The sly-ugg had made a getaway!

Raek called for the prison guards. 'Make them tell us where it is! Make them give it back!' Raek shouted. The guards ordered Crystal and Effie to take off their cloaks and shake out their skirts but there was no sign of the sly-ugg anywhere.

'You don't think I'd allow that horrible thing on me, do you?' Crystal said. 'It's disgusting!'

'I don't know what you're capable of doing to save yourself,' Raek said. But finally he had to give up the search and admit that the sly-ugg had vanished. 'We will find it. I'll put out an alert. What *it* knows, *I* must know!'

He marched out. Everyone breathed a sigh of relief.

'I'm not ill,' Effie said as she kissed Crystal goodbye. 'It's just that the ice is melting. My brain is thawing. Don't worry, my dear daughter. When I remember everything, when I know where to go, nothing will stop us from returning home.'

Effie's eyes shone brilliantly, sparkling as if the sun were reflected in them. Her cheeks were flushed.

'Everything will become clear.'

15

Questrid Has Some Very Small Visitors

The girl at the bottom of the lake had vanished. All Questrid could see was the circle of dirty water far below and the twisted trees round it. He was cold and his hands, jacket cuffs and the end of his scarf were all soaking.

He gave up, scrambled onto the ice and lifted the raft out of the water behind him.

The stone acorn holder lay where it had landed. Questrid picked it up.

'What an absolutely exquisite object,' he said out loud. 'A work of pure genius! I wonder which talented young sculptor could have made it?' He chuckled. 'I have never seen anything so totally brilliant!'

He carefully unscrewed the acorn from the cup. He was not surprised to find a strip of paper inside but he wasn't expecting to see the messages written on it:

I'm forever waiting for you. Hope never dies.
Greenwood. XXX

And on the other side, written in different handwriting:

HELP ME!

Was that message from the girl he'd seen? HELP ME!
Well, of course he would!

He left the raft at the lake's edge, out of the way
amongst some rocks in case he needed it again, and raced
home on the sledge. However sick Greenwood was, he had
to speak with him. He had to! That girl down there needed
help.

As Questrid came to the last long slope that would take
him home, he caught sight of something high up in the sky
and stopped. It was big. Was it a snow albatross? A mountain macaw? He shielded his eyes against the sun . . . and
stared and stared. A spark of excitement, a little thrill rippled through him. Could it be . . .? It did look like – Yes! It
was! It was a *dragon*! And unless he was badly mistaken,
it was the pixicles' dragon, Boldly Seer!

The enormous purple and silvery dragon came closer
and closer. It swooped low over Questrid, beating the snow
into a storm cloud around him with its wings.

'*Boldly Seer!*' Questrid shouted, waving his arms.
'*Boldly Seer!*'

The dragon circled gracefully one way, then the other, in
a perfect figure of eight, before flying off towards Spindle
House.

Seated on the dragon's back were two small figures. Questrid recognized the red-hatted figure when it waved back to him. 'Little Squitcher!' he yelled. 'Hello!'

The pixicles had meant to name the dragon Boadicea, after the fierce female warrior who rode chariots, but they'd got it a bit wrong and she was Boldly Seer. Questrid had ridden on her himself. He loved dragons. He dreamed of becoming a Dragon Master one day.

Boldly Seer sailed down the hill like a kite and Questrid followed almost as fast on his sledge. When they reached the flat ground, the dragon tucked up her feet and skidded neatly on her belly towards the gateway. At the final moment, just before she hit the wall, she spun round so it was her plump side that gently bumped the stones.

By the time Questrid reached them, the two ice pixicles were climbing down from the seat on Boldly Seer's back and shaking off the snow from their clothes. They were only a little taller than knee-high, very pale-skinned and fair-haired.

'Hello!' Questrid yelled. 'Hello!' He swerved to a halt beside them and jumped off his sledge, dropping down to his knees to be level with them. 'How fantastic to see you! What are you doing here?'

'Greetings, Lanky Boy!' Squitcher took off his red woolly hat and held out a tiny hand, like a mouse paw, to be shaken.

'Welcome to Spindle House!' Questrid said, trying not to crush the minuscule fingers. 'Great to see you – and Boldly Seer.'

'Ah yes, she is remembering you,' Squitcher said. 'You helped her before and a dragon never forgets – did you see how she play dive-bombed you? Oh yes, she remembers you and likes you too.'

The older pixicle stepped forward to shake hands. He had a tiny blob of a white beard on the end of his pointed chin, and crinkled-up translucent grey eyes. When he snatched off his blue hat, a cloud of puffy white hair billowed out.

'Grampy, at your service,' he said.

'Would you like to come inside?' Questrid asked them. 'It's lovely and warm and—'

'No, no!' squeaked Grampy. 'We are not warm-loving pixies!'

'Sorry. I wasn't thinking.'

'Don't snap, Grampy,' Squitcher said. 'The Lanky Boy is only trying to be politely-respectful, aren't you?'

'Yes,' Questrid said. 'It's great to see you and I just thought we should go somewhere more *comfortable*...' He was beginning to shiver because although he didn't usually mind the cold, parts of him had been wet for ages and now he was kneeling in the snow so his knees were wet too.

'We have come on a mission of greatly meaningful-importance,' Squitcher said gravely. 'If you are icy-cold and not comfortable at the present time, we must wait.'

'Why don't you come into the courtyard? You could sit on the bench? Oriole can probably find something for you to eat while I go and change clothes.'

'A jolly-sounding jolly good idea!' Squitcher said. 'Boldly Seer is digging herself a nice bed-nest there by the wall. She will be fine for the night.'

'*Night?*'

Squitcher smiled and raised his eyebrows questioningly. 'Perhaps-maybe. We'll see.'

While the pixicles settled down on the bench in the snow, Questrid explained to Robin and Oriole who their visitors were. Thunder and Lightning stopped munching hay and watched them with interest; they'd never seen anything like a pixicle before. Silver trotted out to sniff them thoroughly and give them a friendly lick.

Oriole handed out cold fizzy drinks and ice cream while Questrid ran up to his room to change. He could barely get his frozen fingers to do up buttons and pull on braces and woolly jumpers. He guessed the visit from the pixicles had to be important – as far as he knew they had never come to Spindle House before.

Wrapped up warmly, a mug of hot chocolate in his hand, he settled down to listen to their story.

'When I was a young slip of a lad,' Grampy began, 'I was a hot-tempered fire-and-brimstone boy.'

'Not like now, then,' Squitcher said with a grin.

'Hush! No joking-mockery matter! My anger was bubbling, boiling, scalding-hot. I see no reason to tell you why or give you details, Lanky Boy, but one day I did a terrible-bad thing . . .' He paused to stroke his pointed ears nervously. 'Oh, the shame, the shame!'

'Never mind all that,' Squitcher said. 'Get on with your story, old man. We're talking hundreds of Marble Mountains years ago. Shame's all gone.'

'You remember our icy eye-cycles in our gardens, don't you?' Grampy asked. 'We are the best ice sculptors for miles around. Our eye-cycles are best-special to us, showing us the future and the gone-away-past. But you may not know that they are priceless-valuable and we never, never let anyone who is a non-pixicle have one. Not ever. Too preciously-special to let others hear a fortune or a pastune, too much danger of someone else-other misusing them and doing bad—'

'I remember you let the girls look in them as a treat when we stayed with you,' Questrid said, 'but I got the feeling they only got a hint at the future—'

'Clever-brainy boy. Face-features do not hint at existence of a working mind. Ha ha! Just my little fun-joke. It's true we can see more in the eye-cycles than any other Water person. Certain-sure more than non-Water types like you. In the wrong hands of the wrong sort, an eye-cycle can be a dangerous thing.

'And this is why we're presently-here,' Grampy said. 'We have heard a fortune singing and ringing and calling out. Another eye-cycle, you understand? Not an eye-cycle in our village, but *another* one—'

'What's this got to do with Grampy's temper?' Questrid interrupted.

'Wait. Listen. We were amazedly-flabbergasted to hear it,' Squitcher said. 'How was this possible? Another eye-cycle! Where? How?'

'So we set out on Boldly Seer to seek it out,' Grampy said. 'Even though I was knowing in my heart where the fortune rang-sang from.'

'Huh, the silly old man! Wouldn't tell us! Wasted all that time!' Squitcher said.

'Humph. Silly young man! You took some long-time-ages to find it,' Grampy retorted quickly.

'Where was it?' Questrid asked them.

'Pol Lake—'

'Pol Lake! How weird, because—'

'Don't interrupt. Pol Lake is hidden in the folds of the Glass Hills, frozen from top-most to bottom-most,' Grampy said. 'From bottom to top it freezes, except for once on a rare-occasional moment when it is not frozen and then a gateway opens and you can slip along through to the other side.'

Questrid thrilled at the words. 'Yes? I know. I mean I sort of know. Where to? Where's the other side?' He could barely speak with excitement.

'I don't know! The other side, that's all I can tell you,' Grampy said quickly. 'I threw the eye-cycle in there to spite my father. I told you I was a fearful, brimstone-temper boy.'

'You threw the eye-cycle into the lake?' Questrid said.

'Yes. And some person has got it down there and they are badly-wickedly employing it. We flew over the lake and saw the melt hole. We heard the eye-cycle singing a fortune; the tune was coming up through the hole—'

'But hold on,' Questrid interrupted him. 'I don't understand. It must be years ago that you threw it in – but only now that you've heard it?'

106

'Oh, Lanky One, what questions and questions!' Grampy said.

'But he deserves a polite answer, Grampy,' Squitcher said. 'We think that when Grampy threw-tossed the eye-cycle into the hole it didn't reach the other side, but got trapped-lodged in the ice. Frozen up and iced there. Maybe for years and years it slowly sank through the ice. I don't know. We thought we heard it ten years-long ago but we weren't sure – there was an ice melting moment then also. Now the melt hole is open again and out comes-singing the sound—'

'Our sound! Our eye-cycle! Someone is using it! This cannot happen,' Grampy said. 'It must be stopped!'

'So that's why we're here,' Squitcher said. 'We need your help to go and find-locate it and bring it back.'

'But, but—'

'You are being a jolly Stone-Wood person,' Squitcher went on. 'You are perfect for passing through. We are ice pixies, yes from the Water tribe, and yes we can pass through, but look at us! So small and minuscule. What could we do down there?'

'And if we *did* go down,' Grampy put in, 'they'd keep us – whoever they are – make us tell what's in the eye-cycle. Not good. Much better *you* go, Lanky Boy. Lanky Boy can't do anything useful with the eye-cycle.'

'Well—'

'So please, dear friend, will you help us?'

16
Trouble for Grint

The power was slipping away from him; Grint could feel it. The Elders he'd spoken to that morning had not looked him in the eye. They had not laughed at his jokes or clapped and cheered as he spoke. How was this possible so suddenly, he wondered? After all he'd done building up the Town. Just one day without Effie and he was already losing control. He should have nipped John Carter's rebelliousness in the bud.

He decided to call a further meeting in an attempt to quieten things down and regain some control.

The Elders grouped in the hall, muttering and whispering. Grint climbed onto a big marble table to speak. He could hear desperation in his voice and tried to slow down his speech and steady himself. He wiped away the sweat that had broken out on his forehead. He had to make them see sense. Otherwise he would lose Effie and he could not afford for that to happen;

not if he was to have any chance of remaining their leader.

'We must all thank Mr John Carter for apprehending Effie and Crystal Waters,' he said, trying to smile through his gritted teeth. Whatever he did, his voice rumbled and grated as if it were tired. 'Mr Carter has been very diligent... I agree that Effie stepped out of line when she tried to leave the Town but—'

'Stealing! Stealing, don't forget!'

'And I know some of her dabbling with herbs and flowers might seem—'

'*Might seem?*' John Carter shouted. 'She killed my cousin, Annie Scott, with her so-called medicine!'

'Now, now, we have no proof—'

'She's not like us,' someone shouted. 'She doesn't look like us. Nor does her daughter. We don't want them here!'

'I fail to understand—'

But the Elders shouted Grint down. 'She's a witch!' John Carter cried. 'We've talked it through. We Elders have consulted and we agree she is a witch and must be tried by us. Maybe she's bewitched you, Grint, Bless and Praise You, maybe that's why you think she's worth saving!'

'We don't want a witch in the Town.'

'She should be put to the witch test!' Sam Smith, Carter's friend, called out. 'Who agrees?'

Everyone in the room raised their arm in agreement.

'No, no!' Grint had to shout to be heard. 'This is just the sort of superstitious rubbish I wanted to eradicate from the Town! She *is* different, but she is not a witch!'

'All right for you to say that!' Henry Timms cried. 'You're protected here in your big house with Raek to look after you, doctors to tend you. We have nothing except the likes of Effie Waters, and if her magic does kill us who do we turn to then, eh?'

'Yes!' another cried. 'She's killed! She'll kill again. I say test her. See if she is a witch!'

'The ducking stool will prove it!'

'The two of them want throwing out of the place,' Sam Smith said. 'They're odd. Never belonged.'

'No, no, not the ducking stool,' Grint said. 'You're wrong! That's from the dark ages. We can't— Haven't I always been right? Don't I know always what will happen? I'm telling you—'

'But now *we're* telling *you*!' John Carter cried. 'This time *we* are making the decision. And if she's not a witch, it won't hardly matter, will it?'

'That's right, because if she's innocent, she'll come up unhurt and if she's guilty, she'll drown!' Henry Timms said.

'Ah, I don't know,' Sam Smith said. 'If she comes up not drowned doesn't that mean she is a witch?'

'Let's just do it!'

'Yeah! The sooner the better,' another man called.

'We'll build the ducking stool right away!' John Carter shouted. 'Come on, men! A good ducking in Lop Lake will soon tell us just what sort of a woman Effie Waters really is!'

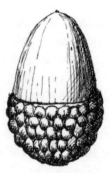

17

A Challenge for Questrid

Questrid hugged his big coat round his shoulders. A wind was blowing up and snow swirled off the stable roof and scattered around them.

'Wow. I need to think about this.' He got up and paced round the yard nervously. 'I can't say I'm not scared, because I am. Go through the melt hole? Wow. What if I drown? Or if I do get through to the other side, what if I never come back?'

The pixicles looked at each other sympathetically, as if it were they who were having this problem. They shrugged.

'Would be a jolly disgracing-shame,' Grampy said. 'Tragic-sad.' He didn't sound sad.

'If only Copper were here,' Questrid said. 'She'd know what to do.'

'Oh, the lovely Coppery person! I am loving her!' Squitcher said, slapping a hand on his knee. 'I am wishing she was here too. She is always having such good ideas.'

'Great. Thanks,' Questrid muttered.

'Oh, Lanky Boy, we are never forgetting your help in the past. Never. And it is you who are here and who we need to help us now. Will you do it?'

'First I must talk to Greenwood. He knows about this lake, but he's . . .'

'The Uncle Greenwood of Spindle Tree House? I have heard Coppery One talk of him. A bendy-wood person, isn't he?'

'Yes. But he started being odd after he went to Pol Lake and there's the acorn and now you come with this story about the eye-cycle . . . They're all connected.'

'Please do go see him. We will not go-leaving you until we have an answer in the jolly affirmative-yes mode,' Squitcher said. 'Then we will go back home with our eye-cycle.' He folded his arms. 'We will wait here.'

'You can't just sit here all night!'

'We will be very jolly,' Squitcher said, smiling. 'All is chilly-well here.'

Questrid gulped. He looked at the two tiny pixicles sitting on the bench swinging their little legs backwards and forwards; both had their beady eyes fixed on him like a pair of pale birds watching their prey.

'You're jolly good with your nose and your eyes,' Squitcher said. 'A tracker. A hunter. You would be finding our precious eye-cycle easily.'

'I don't know. I don't know.'

'Well, we will sit and wait,' Grampy said, taking a swig of his fizzy drink. 'You are the one we choose. Thank you.'

'Oh, please—'

'Coppery One would not be taking so long thinking this one out,' Squitcher said, playing with a ball of snow. 'But then she's very clever-brainy, is she not?'

Questrid jumped up and brushed the snow off his coat. 'I'll go see Greenwood now.'

He knocked on Greenwood's door. 'I'm sorry to disturb you,' he called out rather breathlessly. 'But I need to ask you something. Are you well enough for me to come in?' He steadied himself against the wooden wall trying to ignore the sway of the tree around him.

'Go away!' Greenwood shouted. 'I need to be alone!'

Questrid went in anyway.

Greenwood was lying on his bed in his dressing gown staring up at the ceiling. He did not look round at Questrid.

'How are you?' Questrid asked gently. He felt embarrassed to see Greenwood reduced to such a feeble figure.

'I'm not here,' Greenwood said weakly.

'Oh.' Questrid stared out through the three windows at the snowy mountains, but the landscape moved as the treetop bent in the wind and he was hit by a wave of sickness. A sudden gust shook the branch so badly that two books fell off Greenwood's desk.

'Happens all the time,' Greenwood said lightly. 'Suppose you feel it more; Stone and Rock in you.'

'You don't look well. I'm sorry to disturb you, but I had to come.' Questrid sat down beside the bed. 'It's about Pol Lake.'

Greenwood sat up sharply. His face was much more lined than Questrid remembered it. 'What? Why? Why *that* lake? Why my darlings and that lake?'

Questrid patted Greenwood's arm and tried to smile reassuringly. 'Greenwood, let me tell you why the pixicles have come and what they want me to do.'

When Greenwood had heard Questrid's story, he swung himself off the bed, stood up and stared through one of the windows. He was trembling. 'That lake is dangerous. I know it is.' He ruffled his hair with a shaking hand. 'Are you asking me to give you permission to go?' he said at last. 'Or are you asking me for some other reason?'

'Greenwood, I'm sorry, really sorry, but I saw you – at the lake . . .' Questrid pulled out the stone acorn holder from his pocket and held it up. 'I saw you throw this into the water—'

Greenwood groaned as he took the acorn from him.

'I did that? I don't remember. You can't trust that lake. You never know what it's up to and its magic is so strong. There are forces at work at Pol Lake that would give you nightmares for the rest of your life!' He paused to look at the acorn. 'I've never seen it before.'

'You have. You threw it—'

'Did I? I did!' Greenwood spun round. 'Quickly, tell me how did you get this? Have you looked inside?' He was already unscrewing the acorn holder with fumbling fingers. He pulled out the slip of paper. When he read, HELP ME, he lurched, as if his legs had snapped. 'No, it can't be! But—' He fell back on the bed. 'How did you . . .? How . . .?'

'Take care! You're ill!'

'A message! A message from her! It must be! How did you get it?'

'I'll tell you. Sit down again. Just listen.'

Questrid described how he'd followed Greenwood to the lake, seen what he did and then how the acorn holder had come back. He described the blonde girl at the other side of the water. Greenwood grabbed Questrid's wrist.

'A *girl*? How old?'

'I don't know. I couldn't say, but—'

'But she was blonde? Really white-blonde?'

Questrid nodded.

'I can't bear it, I truly can't bear it,' Greenwood moaned. 'It's easier to be confused. Confused and frozen solid rather than this! To be so close!'

Questrid didn't understand him so he went on: 'And now,' he said, 'the pixicles want me to go down there, through the melt hole and—'

'Yes, you must! You must!'

'The pixicles want me to find their lost eye-cycle and I don't know if I dare but that girl – I think she needs help too and—'

'Oh, but yes, yes, *you* could do it!' Greenwood interrupted. 'You could find them. You could do it. We don't have long. Pol Lake will freeze over again – if it hasn't already. That will be the end. The last time they can escape for years and years...'

'Who? That girl with the blonde hair?'

'Yes. That's Crystal, my daughter.'

* * *

115

'Years ago I had a family of my own... When I found you lost on the mountains, covered in snow, Questrid, half-frozen and weeping for your mother, it was almost as if I was being given another chance to be a father... But I don't think I took it, did I? I couldn't. I was frozen, struck with splinters of ice in my heart, ever since they disappeared...

'We were out exploring; Fountain my wife, Crystal and I. Crystal was about one and a half, such a dear, dear poppet! I'd just finished a wood-picture for her – a picture of us three... We found Pol Lake by chance and we were so enchanted! Hah! *Enchanted* is the right word, I now think! I should have sensed how strong its forces were. We walked out on the ice. We could see straightaway that it was all frozen except in the middle where it was the clearest brightest turquoise blue. We'd never seen anything like it. Effie, that's what I called my dear Fountain, was pulled to it, as if it were a magnet. I called out to her to take care, she was holding the baby in her arms, but she kept on going towards it. Something was wrong. I felt a tension in the air, a sort of *snapping*... like jaws... "Something's calling me," she told me. "Can you hear it?" I couldn't hear anything. "Come away!" I yelled, but I dared not run. I could feel the ice cracking under the soles of my boots. She tilted her head to listen – not to me, but to something else, something I couldn't hear. She looked so pretty with the sun glinting on her blonde head, her little elfish chin... She went closer and closer to the water. I told her again to keep away. The place was magic. Dangerous. I felt those jaws coming closer, ready to bite.

I called her back. I went towards her. I didn't think... But she was being pulled, Questrid, dragged by some great force down there! Before I could reach her, she leaped in – into the water! There was no splash, nothing. She just disappeared. She vanished as if she'd never existed at all and took our baby with her.

'Oh, Questrid, I haven't been able to remember that terrible incident for years and years... They both slipped through the water as if they were slipping through a tear in a sheet of silk... and that was the last I saw of her: of both of them. It's as if I've been stuck in some awful long sleep with no dreams and no thoughts and nothing but emptiness...'

'I'm so sorry,' Questrid said. 'I don't know what to say. It's terrible. It's—'

'Yes, terrible. I knew it was magic, and I tried to fight it. I was certain they weren't dead. I *knew* they were not dead. I'd heard of a Gateway to the World Below... We'd heard Grint was down there. He'd loved Effie once... But I couldn't get through the Gateway. I tried. I'm all Wood, Questrid, as you know, and although Wood folk can swim since they float easily, they cannot dive. Cannot pass *through* water.'

'But couldn't another Water person have gone down and brought them back?' Questrid asked.

'Yes, yes, but there were no Water people for miles and miles that I knew of! Effie herself comes from far away over the other side of Malachite Mountain. And I had no time. I tried to dive but I bobbed up like a cork. I put rocks in my pockets to weigh me down but it was useless. I came back to the lake with Stone people and Water people as soon as I could, but the Gateway was nearly closed; the ice was creeping around, sealing it off. And I'd grown confused so I had great difficulty explaining myself. When the melt hole closed up finally, I did too. I shut down. All I knew was that Fountain and Crystal were lost to me. We tried to break up the ice, we tried everything but nothing worked—'

'Until?'

'That day you followed me. You see I often went there without knowing why, but on that occasion I could remember Effie's leaving. It was because the Gateway was open. I had your acorn – I'm sorry, I'd picked it up admiring it and pocketed it by mistake. There was a slip of paper in it – as if you knew! I wrote a few words and I threw it in. I hurried back to get help but I fell ill – the place is cursed, enchanted, whatever you might call it, and I've been out of my mind ever since.'

'The Gateway is still open,' Questrid said, leaning forward encouragingly.

Greenwood's eyes gleamed.

'We have a chance!'

18
Questrid Takes the Plunge

Crystal lingered outside the prison, staring up at the barred windows, wondering if her mother were behind one of them. The prison building, which she'd never looked closely at before, was well kept with a good roof and stout doors. Typical of Grint to maintain the prison, she thought.

Eventually she made her way back to their block through the grim dusty streets. Without her mum she felt light and unreal and incomplete.

The empty carry-box bumping lightly against her thigh reminded her of her promise to protect the sly-ugg. She'd failed. It had vanished. She was doubly alone.

She glanced over her shoulder nervously, looking up the road towards the Square. Grint needed Effie, but no one needed her. Would someone try and get rid of her? She'd better lock herself inside tonight, bolt the door; arm herself with a knife . . .

Her block was all dark and forbidding. She couldn't go in. She turned away and climbed up towards the trees surrounding Lop Lake.

She almost stopped breathing when she saw what had been done there.

On the far side where the ground was clear of rocks, the Town Guard had begun to erect a ducking machine. It made Crystal feel sick to see it. It consisted of a long metal arm, like a seesaw, from which a chair dangled. Men pulling on the rope would swing it out over the dirty lake water and then drop it down or haul it up from the water.

It will not happen. It cannot happen, Crystal told herself. It is too horrible. Inhuman. Something will stop it. I know it will. It must!

'Help me!' she whispered to the flat grey water of Lop Lake. 'I asked you for help – I sent the acorn. Greenwood, whoever you are, help me!'

She felt a sudden twist in the air; something seemed to snap.

She stepped back, watching the water all the time, knowing something was going to happen.

Right in the centre of the lake a bubble slowly surfaced and erupted with a burping sound. She heard a distant, surging rumble. Ripples ringed out one upon another all the way to her feet, and sent the water lap-lapping against the shore.

Something's coming! Something's coming!

It was a boy. He shot out of the water as if he'd been fired from a cannon, sailing through the air in a gigantic arc. His long scarf trailed behind him like a banner. He landed with a bone-crunching crash on the ground beside her and lay immobile for several long moments. Just when Crystal decided he was definitely dead, he got slowly to his feet.

'Wow!' He was grinning from ear to ear. 'It worked! I'm not even damp!' He picked up his fallen hat. 'Wow!'

Crystal was surprised and not surprised. She'd wanted someone to come and they had. 'Greenwood?' she said.

Questrid shook his head. 'No. Are you Crystal?'

She had never seen anyone with such twinkling eyes nor such a smiley face. She nodded.

'My name's Questrid. I'm from the other side. The Marble Mountains. Gosh, it's warm down here, isn't it?' He unwound his scarf and took off his gloves.

She knew he must be waiting for her to speak but she couldn't say a word.

'I got your message,' Questrid added, grinning. 'It was you, wasn't it? You want help?'

Crystal fought back the tears that were threatening to ruin everything. She nodded.

'Well, here I am. Questrid, at your service!' and he gave her a mock bow.

'Where's the Greenwood person?' she said at last, looking at the water as if expecting him to fly out too.

'He couldn't come. He sent me.' He held out the acorn holder. 'He sent this so you'd know I was his messenger.'

'I want Greenwood,' Crystal said.

'I'm sorry, I'll try and explain.' Questrid looked round for somewhere to sit and suddenly saw the awfulness of

121

his surroundings. 'Wow! What a dump! Is there anywhere a bit nicer we could go?'

Crystal nodded and walked back towards her block. 'This way.'

Questrid followed, staring round at the deserted ruined buildings. There were few lights, pathetic little trees, weedy flowers. No snow. He'd had nightmares that were more fun than this. The only good thing about this place was the lack of people – no one around to notice his arrival.

'This is where I live.' Crystal opened the door of their apartment.

'I see.' He looked round at the bare room. 'It's lovely,' he said. 'Is grey the *in* colour down here, then?'

Crystal looked puzzled. 'What do you mean?'

'Nothing, nothing, just— Nothing.'

Questrid shivered and huddled closer to the fire. It wasn't cold, not compared to the mountains, but the atmosphere was dank, like being in a cellar, and he felt chilled to his bones in this room.

'Do you live here alone?'

'With my mum, but—' She couldn't tell him yet.

'What's it called, this place?'

'This is just our block in the Town.'

'Right.'

'How did you come through the water?' Crystal asked at last. 'Why didn't Greenwood come? Who is he, this Greenwood?'

'You don't know? I wonder what you *do* know? Greenwood's your— ' He stopped, suddenly realizing just

122

how shocking his news was going to be. 'You'd better prepare yourself, Crystal. I've got a lot to tell you.'

Crystal sat very still while he told her what he had learned from Greenwood. She didn't interrupt or question him but let him tell the whole story in one go.

'It's hard to believe. To suddenly learn that I have a father...' Her chin quivered. 'To know where I come from, after all this time...'

'I know, I had a similar experience when I found I had a mother. And I found out I was half Rock and there I was living with all these Wood people and they hated each other – the Woods and the Rocks, I mean. Really weird.'

A hint of a smile flickered over Crystal's face. 'So you understand a bit how I feel?'

Questrid nodded. 'You feel all undone, that's what Copper would say. *Unravelled!* Yes, finding you have a new parent is really weird. I don't feel like other people feel about their mums,' he admitted. 'Ruby, my mum, is kind and funny and clever, but I suppose I just don't know her and we don't live together... One day, maybe we'll be closer... But I love everyone at Spindle House—'

Crystal jumped. 'Oh, Mum talked about a spindle tree!'

'Did she? It really is a tree – a massive one. Everyone lives in it except me. I live in the stable and I have a metal bed. And I like the horses. But listen, we can't just sit here chatting,' Questrid said, getting up and pacing around. 'We have to—'

'And is there snow and ice and snowflakes and is it clean and is there clear water?'

Questrid laughed. 'Yes. All that.'

123

'Oh, I want to go there! How will we get there? How can we get Mum there—' Her voice broke. 'You've come too late, Questrid! They've locked Mum in prison and they're going to do some horrible thing to her – a trial to prove, to prove that she's a witch...'

'A *witch*?'

'Of course she isn't,' Crystal said.

'Of course not. It *is* old-fashioned down here, isn't it? Medieval even!' Questrid said. 'But, listen, to do this horrid test will mean they have to take her out of prison. When she's not locked up we at least have a chance of rescuing her. Let's hope they do it soon.'

'*What?*'

'Crystal, listen, I don't know how long the Gateway will be open. A day? Less than a day? We need to get out of here, all three of us, as quickly as possible. To get back to the other side – to get us *home* – we have to go back into that horrid dirty water, right through the middle of it – off a boat or a raft or something – but first... The pixicles' eye-cycle! Where is it? I've got to steal it.' He grinned at Crystal. 'Hey, this is turning out quite exciting, isn't it?'

Crystal shook her head. 'The eye-cycle is in Grint's house, probably locked up. We'll never get it.'

'Course we will. Now, before we get started, have you got anything I could eat? I'm starving!'

19
Patient Pixicles

Grampy and Squitcher sat cross-legged on the ice, staring into the still, clear water of Pol Lake.

'Not a splash,' Squitcher said, shaking his head gently. 'Like he was jumping through an invisible hole.'

'Maybe he was. Brave boy,' Grampy said.

'It's your faulty-blunder that he's had to go down there!' Squitcher snapped. He was worried about Questrid.

'But now he is doing a good thing for Greenwood too,' Grampy said calmly. 'We've both made mistakes and the Lanky One is putting them right. That is like magic. Real magic.'

They were silent again. Then ...

'Do you hear something?' Squitcher said, cocking his head on one side. 'A scritching noise? Scratching. Icifying.'

Grampy smoothed his little hand over the ice. 'Yes. Ice is creeping-growing,' he said. 'It's coming sneaking in.'

The blue circle was getting smaller.

Squitcher nodded. 'Our Lanky Boy hasn't got much time.'

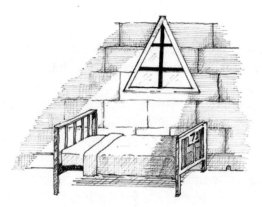

20

How Sly is a Sly-ugg?

Effie stared at the grey walls and the metal bed of her prison cell. Not so bad, rather like home, she thought with a small smile.

A key screeched in the lock and Grint came into the cell. 'Wait outside,' he ordered the guard.

Effie ignored him and stared out of the barred window at the clouds.

'Effie.' Grint pulled up a stool close beside her and studied her profile silently for a long time. 'I don't want to keep you in here,' he told her. 'I didn't want this to happen. The Elders and Raek – especially Raek, they don't understand. They insist you undergo this ordeal. I can't stop them. I have little power while I haven't got you and the eye-cycle working for me.'

Effie shrugged at the window.

'I expect you'll be all right,' he added. 'I *know* you'll be all right – Effie, are you listening to me? It might help to know this... You are from the Water Clan and water can't harm you. You need not worry about drowning. You're not a witch. You'll be fine.'

Effie's shoulders stiffened. '*Water Clan?*' she repeated.

'Yes. You're a Water person. Water – that fluid stuff, you know. Don't you remember anything about the past?'

'I do. Something has shifted and my brain is clearing. Yes!' She spun round. '*You* are from the Stone Clan! It's coming back, slowly, bits and pieces. You pulled me down here! You kidnapped us!'

Grint grinned. 'How alive you are all of a sudden! You seem to gush, just like your name – *Fountain*! Remember your old name? Yes, I called you down here, I reeled you in like a fish through the ice, through the Gateway, to read the eye-cycle. Greenwood didn't deserve you, I'd always admired you...'

'*Greenwood?* What's that? I left something behind,' Effie said, looking round her cell as if it might be there. She plucked at her skirt. 'I left something important, but I don't remember what. I remember the snow and the cold and the snowflakes falling so fast you couldn't see and the sun glinting on the ice...'

'The Marble Mountains. It was my home too,' Grint said. 'Sometimes I think about that place... But Granite – my so-called friend and cousin who now abides in Malachite Mountain – he took everything! The thieving, skiving, conniving rat! He left me no choice!' He stopped; got up and strode round the cell. When he sat down again he took a deep breath. 'Let's not talk about him. I had to get away and make my own empire. And here it is. The Town was a perfect place to set up. Everything I needed was here, and when the eye-cycle appeared by chance, well, better and better. Only I couldn't see the fortunes. I needed a reader, didn't I? A pixicle or a Water person.'

'A pixicle would die here,' Effie said, still looking outside.

'Quite. But a Water person, like you, wouldn't. You were fine. And now it's all ruined. I need you to read the eye-cycle. I will have no power unless you do. You *have* to survive the ducking, Effie, you must!'

Effie smiled dreamily. 'Have you forgotten, Morton Grint, that if I drown I am innocent, but if I survive it proves I'm a witch and they will burn me at the stake. Either way you won't have me!'

'I will. I'll think of something—'

They heard voices and scuffling noises outside. The door suddenly opened and Raek burst in. The skin on his face was a fiery red and covered with spots.

'What do you want?' Grint snapped, facing Raek defiantly. 'I am questioning the prisoner. You have no right to barge in!'

'Excuse me,' Raek said, 'I only came to see... I was looking for – aha!' He lunged at Effie who cowered back, afraid. 'Don't be scared!' Raek cried. 'I just wanted *this*!' He pulled her shawl off with a flourish, revealing the sly-ugg curled on her chest like a large orange-coloured brooch.

Raek grabbed the sly-ugg and held it up by its tail end. It dangled from his hand, twisting and coiling.

'It went missing in the visiting room, Grint. It had to be hiding somewhere,' Raek said. 'You'll pay for this, Sly-ugg!' He shook it until the sly-ugg's eyes were spinning and it had turned a sickly green.

'I didn't know it was there,' Effie said. 'I swear I didn't!'

'No?' Raek rammed the sly-ugg into the carry-box he'd brought. 'Perhaps not. I'll soon see when I read its miserable little mind.' He stormed out of the cell but was back again almost instantly. 'Oh, Effie, thought you'd like to know; we're going to put you to the drowning test first thing tomorrow morning. Sleep well – *Witch*!' The door slammed behind him.

'Tomorrow? Well, I'm glad I shan't be staying here much longer,' Effie said. 'The bed is really very narrow.'

'Don't joke about it, Effie!' Grint got up and went to the door. 'You will survive the ducking and then I shall have to make sure they stop this persecution. You will not drown, Effie, but don't imagine there is any escape from me. I will never let you go!'

Raek hurried back to Grint's house swinging the carry-box roughly. The sly-ugg bounced and somersaulted and its eye-stalks bumped and bent against the sides.

Raek went straight to his laboratory and put the crumpled sly-ugg into the squeeze-box. The sly-ugg screamed like a banshee but Raek barely heard it, he was so intent on getting every morsel from his spy.

'My dear slime-ball, keep still, keep still. How gooey you are today! You know I'll get it all out of you in the end. Best to give it up quickly. Don't fight it. Come on. Come on, you snotty little slug; cough it up. Spit it out!'

At last the sly-ugg gave up its struggle. A stillness settled over it and it began to glow and shine. Very soon a white circle appeared on the wall and Raek watched it with a dreamy expression.

'Good, good sluggy. Now what did Grint, Bless and Praise his Rotten Name, say to Effie in that cell? Come on.' He squeezed the screws tighter. 'Spit it out!'

Raek did not see the sly-ugg swivel its eyes round and glare at Raek with a most particular look; if he had he might have been more careful.

Effie and Grint appeared in the white circle. Raek listened intently as their conversation was replayed. He jumped up and down when he heard how Grint was from the Marble Mountains.

'Always knew he was different,' Raek said. 'A Stone person, whatever that is. From beyond the Lake – Marble Mountains, eh? This is good information, very useful. My spy is spying on the Master, the Great and Wonderful Morton Grint, Rot and Blast his Stinking Person!'

The soundtrack began to crack and bleep. Raek shook the squeezing machine. 'Pull yourself together, Sly-ugg!'

Grint's voice was cracked and slurred so it was hard to hear the words.

Raek heard his own name. He leaned close to the sly-ugg, straining to catch every word. 'I will save you, Effie . . . You and I will be together . . . witchcraft . . . I will kill Raek... throw him into the swamp... or a skweener... end of them!'

Raek was listening so intently that he did not notice the sly-ugg had turned a startling shade of pink and was now panting with the effort of the image it had produced. Its eye-stalks drooped. It was drenched in slime.

Raek knew very little about sly-uggs, and cared less. He did not know that when pushed to its limit a sly-ugg could invent images and distort language.

A sly-ugg could lie.

'So Grint plans to get rid of me, does he?' Raek said out loud. He paced round the table. 'Double-crosser! Well, not before I get rid of *him*. I'll show him I'm smarter than he is! I've got you, Sly-ugg. And I'll get that eye-cycle thing too. I'll steal it and then he won't be able to use it. I bet I can see into it myself if I try. I'll get Crystal to do it. I bet she can. Then I will be the new leader of the Town! Hail Raek, Worship and Honour his Wonderful Name!'

He released the screws and the sly-ugg flopped weakly onto the table like a wet sock.

'What's wrong with you?' Raek dropped the sly-ugg into a velvet drawstring bag. 'Bit over squeezed? Sorree! In you go and stay there.' He pulled the strings tight. 'I haven't finished with you yet! I'm going to plant you on Grint and you must spy on him. One-step-ahead Raek, that's me!'

21
Are Witches Waterproof?

Questrid was standing at the apartment door with his hand on the doorknob. 'We must go and find the eye-cycle. Now!'

'We can't,' Crystal said. 'There's a night curfew. The Town Guard would pick us up straightaway. There's nothing we can do till morning.' She popped a Minty Moment into her mouth and offered him one. 'Sorry, I can't stop eating these – my last few.'

'They're not very nice,' Questrid said. 'We have much tastier things in the Marble Mountains. Snowbombs. Icepoppers. Mountain Mints.' He paced round the room sucking the sweet. 'We can't do *nothing*!'

'We wouldn't stand a chance at night. There! Listen!' They both went still and concentrated as the marching feet suddenly clattered down the road outside. 'There they are! The Town Guard,' Crystal told him. 'All night. Every night.'

'Well then, tomorrow, really early, as soon as it's light,' Questrid said. 'But the lake may be frozen over by then. It's nerve-racking! I'll never sleep.'

'We'll go first thing. But what about Mum? I still don't...'

'Don't worry. We will save her.' Questrid marvelled at his own words. He was only working on the merest thread of evidence: that because Effie was a Water person, she would not drown. Beyond that, he was leaving everything to chance.

Questrid spent the rest of the evening telling Crystal about the Marble Mountains, Spindle House and all the people who lived in it and how they were related.

'I'm Stone and Wood,' Questrid said. 'In the olden days the clans never intermarried, but they do now. Wood and Stone. Water and Bird. As Greenwood's daughter you must be half Wood and half–'

'*His* daughter? It sounds so weird when all I've ever been is *her* daughter... I do love the trees and wooden furniture... When I sit on one of Grint's wooden chairs it feels like it knows me or something! So silly, isn't it?'

'Not at all silly, that sensation is quite normal for someone like you. Me too, though my Wood side is sort of underdeveloped somehow.'

'And do I *look* normal to you too?'

'Sure. Why not?'

'I'd fit in up there in the Marble Mountains? You see, no one else in the Town has blue eyes and blonde hair. They're all dark, or at least no one is so fair as we are. And Mum and I are different in other ways too, it's hard to define, but – but when I talk to you I don't feel so different. You understand...'

'Yes. I understand because I'm from the Mountains and we both come from a mixed tribe family. Effie's real name is Fountain. She's a Water person and so, as I was trying to tell you earlier, your other half must be Water.'

'Yes!' Crystal cried. 'Mum was trying to tell me that when I went to see her – but I was too distracted to take it all in. We're even called Waters and I love water, even dirty Lop Lake!'

'When you're back on the other side,' Questrid said, 'you'll feel at home – it's all water there, though most of it's frozen.'

Questrid woke slowly. He could hear hammering outside and men's voices. He rolled over and tried to go back to sleep but then, remembering where he was, he jumped out of bed. He'd slept in Effie's metal bed, but still he hadn't slept well. There was too much to worry about, and all through the night the sound of the Town Guard had disturbed him. He shook his head, longing for a blast of clean, fresh Marble Mountain air.

Crystal was standing at the window. Questrid could see she'd been crying.

'They're finishing the chair. Look!' She was trembling. 'Poor Mum. It's awful! We must stop them! We'll have to go up there... how will I bear it?'

Questrid tried to pat her shoulder but it didn't seem quite right to touch her. 'It's impossible for Effie to drown.' He hoped he was right. 'Now, could you give me something to wear that might make me look like I belong here? I've got to look like a Towner.'

He had already taken off his long, colourfully striped scarf. Crystal gave him an old felt cap that someone had left at the apartment and a short black scarf to go round his neck.

'Better take some food,' he said as Crystal headed for the door. 'I mean, we don't know when we'll get a chance to eat.'

Crystal made an '*are you crazy*?' face at him but helped him gather some stuff. They put all they could find – bread, sweets, apples and a bun – in their pockets.

People were gathering round the lake. The air was filled with the smell of wet leaves and decay and damp from where their feet had disturbed the earth. When Crystal and Questrid got there, the Towners moved away from them as if they were contaminated. No one noticed that Questrid was a stranger.

Grint arrived. Usually he was greeted with cheers and the children waved at him, but today there were only a few muttered whispers of 'Grint, Bless and Praise your Name!' They knew he was losing power.

Grint marched across to a boulder and climbed up to address everyone. 'People! My people!' he called out in his rumbling gravelly voice. 'It is not too late for you to change your minds about this. Effie Waters is not a witch. Who amongst you really believes that she is? She is a kind person; many of you have used her medicines and got better as a result. Many of you have put her creams on your burns and cuts and been cured. Are we going to dump her in that dirty water just because one patient wasn't so lucky? We don't need these outdated customs and superstitions. We are above this!'

'He's trying to save her!' Questrid whispered to Crystal.

'No, he's trying to save himself!' Crystal shot back. 'He knows he can't use the eye-cycle without her. He'd say anything. Anything. The toad!'

'Don't I, your leader, give you what you want?' Grint went on. 'You are safe here. You have food and shelter. We are not under attack . . . I am a good leader. I have always predicted rebellions and—'

'Yes!' someone cried from the crowd, 'but maybe that's because you have a WITCH visit you and tell you what's going on!'

The crowd jeered. 'Witch! Witch!'

'There is no such thing as witchcraft!' Grint yelled. 'This ridiculous charade will get us nowhere, we—'

'You said there was witchcraft a few days ago,' Sam Smith said.

'Yeah!'

'Be quiet, Grint!'

'Yeah, shut up!'

'We want the ducking!'

'Look! Here they come!'

The entire crowd, which had been growing bigger moment by moment, turned to watch Raek and the Town Guard bring Effie up to the lake.

Effie was not wearing a hood. Her white-blonde hair hung down to her shoulders in a cloud of shimmery silvery-gold. The Guards escorting her kept a few paces away as if they were scared to touch her. Raek held her firmly by the arm.

There were shouts and boos from the Towners as the little troupe drew closer. 'Witch!' 'Sorceress!' 'Murderer!'

Effie was calm. Her eyes tracked round the circle of faces, looking for Crystal. When their eyes met she smiled and held out her arms. Crystal ran and hugged her and the guards didn't stop her.

'Mum, Mum! Are you all right?' Then, burrowing her head in her mother's shoulder, she whispered, '*Greenwood!* Do you remember Greenwood? He's from the other side. He sent a boy – Questrid. He says you can't drown. You can't! Mum, do you hear me?'

Raek pulled them apart roughly.

'Stop that!' he squawked. 'That's enough!'

Crystal struggled to keep her arms round her mother. She had to hold her as long as she could in case Questrid was wrong and this was the last time. She tightened her grip.

Raek tried to prise them apart but the guards didn't help.

'Don't just stand there!' Raek shouted as he pulled and pushed at the mother and daughter. 'Help me! She's not going to harm you! She can't put a spell on you, if that's what you're worried about.'

Inside Raek's pocket, the sly-ugg was wriggling around in the velvet bag. It had worked itself free and now quickly it inched amongst the folds of Effie's dress. Once hidden, it clung on and didn't move.

Raek and the guards finally separated Crystal from her mother. They took Effie to the chair and strapped her in.

Crystal found Questrid at her side.

'Don't worry,' he whispered. 'Don't cry. You'll see the chair go under but she'll be fine. If only she weren't tied in, she might even get through the Gateway, like I did, because the ducking chair reaches right into the middle... But if she doesn't, then she'll come up a bit wet and then they'll untie her and we can grab her—'

'How? You're just making this up! You don't know anything, do you? You only hope!'

'True... I'm hoping the Gateway isn't icing up, too.'

Effie ignored the crowd who were calling out to her and jeering. Even Stella was there, shaking her fist. Effie was calm. She didn't flinch as the men strapped a leather belt round her waist; she showed no fear at all. She might have been going to plunge into a pool of crystal clear liquid – not the dirty grey muck of Lop Lake.

When they'd secured her and she was sitting alone in the chair, the crowd fell quiet as if they suddenly realized what a terrible thing they were doing.

'Oh dear, poor Effie.'

'What a to-do.'

Four men hoisted the chair into the air where it jigged about awkwardly. Crystal groaned and cried out. All eyes swivelled round and looked at her, then swivelled back to the seat swaying above the ground.

'Eh, I'm not sure it's the right thing,' Mrs Jones said quietly.

'I never thought she was a witch,' Mrs Brown said. 'She was too kind and clever. Too dreamy. Nothing good will come of this! What about poor Crystal? What'll become of her?'

The four men pulled on the rope and the long arm suspending the chair went out over the water. They stopped when it reached the very centre of the lake.

'You have one last chance to change your minds, people of the Town!' Grint cried suddenly. Everyone turned and looked at him again. 'Effie Waters is innocent. She is not a witch. You know she is not! Save her from this terrible ordeal! Let's think of another punishment we can give her. Not this here, not at this muddy hole of Lop Lake!'

John Carter elbowed up to the front and faced Grint. 'Why are you so keen to save her, Grint, Bless and Praise your Name?' he asked. 'You've always agreed before about banning witchcraft. What's changed?'

'Yeah, why's she so special?'

'Duck her!'

'Duck her!'

'Drown her!'

Effie didn't hear the crowd roaring. She didn't see anything. The name *Greenwood* was ringing and singing in her head and a vague, blurred picture of him was growing stronger all the time. She was glad and hopeful without knowing why.

Effie snapped out of her dream suddenly when the sly-ugg moved. It was slithering out from under her shawl and onto her lap. It slimed beneath the free end of the strap round her waist. Effie bit back a cry. What was it doing? She did not think it would harm her... was it trying to help her? She didn't dare look at the sly-ugg, knowing the crowd was watching everything closely. She tried to look at the water, the sky, anything; meanwhile she felt the sly-ugg arching its rubbery body, pushing and straining against the leather.

'On the count of three,' Raek yelled. 'One! Two!'

Effie was right. The sly-ugg was trying to help her. It worked faster and faster, forcing the buckle to undo and release the strap. It grew pink with effort, wheezing and whimpering with worry as it pushed and pushed . . .

'THREE!'

The chair dropped into the water with a mighty splash.

The lake seemed to rip open and waves rippled up and sucked at the bank. Dark evil bubbles of stinking gas exploded. Twiggy branches, empty bottles and plastic bags swirled around and spun in crazy circles. Dirty water and sodden leaves sprayed out over the watching people who screamed and stumbled backwards, giggling nervously and shouting out.

Crystal buried her face in her hands. 'Mum, Mum!'

'I'm sorry,' Questrid whispered. 'Seeing that must be so awful for you. Horrid. But I really think she's all right, I really do and – Oh, Crystal please, could we go?'

'What? Are you mad?'

'It would be the perfect moment. While everyone's here.'

'I don't care! I don't care about the stupid eye-cycle! I want my mum. We can't go and just leave her. Is she alive? Where is she?'

Time passed very slowly. The crowd began to mutter and whisper.

'How long is the chair to stay down?' John Carter asked.

'That's enough,' Grint called. His voice sounded broken. 'No one could survive that!'

'Bring her up!' Mrs Brown cried. 'Bring her up!'

Raek checked his watch and raised his arm. He held it poised as he stared at his watch. At last he waved to the men to lift up the chair. They pulled on the rope. Everyone surged forward again to look.

Slowly the rope emerged, dripping and slimy, then the top of the chair covered with weed. There was a murmur around the lake. Then a spit-spat of angry voices, sharp words and cries...

The chair was empty.

22

'Are you perhaps Fountain?'

'Something's coming!' Grampy cried, staring hard at the meltwater. 'I'm feeling it in my skeleton-bones and it's jolly thrilling-exciting!'

Whatever it was, it was approaching them fast, with a sound like a ski rasping on ice, or the whirr of a fish hauled in on a line. A brilliant flash of light and a *POP!* sent them both toppling over.

A figure flew out of the water. It came tumbling down on the ice beside them in a flurry of long cloak and blonde hair. The pixicles scrambled to their feet and hurried over.

'It's a woman!' Grampy said, kneeling beside her.

'And not a drop of water on her white-lovely skin, or her cloaky-clothes or her silvery-blonde hair!' Squitcher said.

The woman lay staring up at the sky blankly. She had intensely blue eyes. The pixicles looked at each other in alarm. Was she dead?

She smiled. She wasn't dead.

'Greetings, pale-person from below the ice,' Grampy said, bowing. He offered his small hand to her and she took it and sat up. 'Welcome. Are you perhaps *Fountain?*'

Effie nodded. She breathed in deeply. 'I am.' She turned her head very slowly, taking in everything she saw: the sheer glassy walls, the sun glittering on the ice, the blue-white snow. She seemed to blossom before their eyes: her cheeks filled out, her skin glowed and her eyes grew rounder, clearer, and as brilliant as sapphires. 'I remember,' she said. 'I've come home. I am Fountain and I'm home at last!'

'Yes and we're jolly, jolly glad to have you back,' Squitcher said. 'I will take you down to Spindle House—'

'Yes, yes – but look, look at the ice!' Grampy cried. 'Listen to it growing!'

The ice was inching over the water like a creamy white brittle skin.

The Gateway was almost closed.

23

Raek's Big Mistake

'The ducking chair's empty!' Crystal cried, turning to Questrid. 'But—'

'Brilliant! I told you she'd make it!' Questrid hugged Crystal then quickly let her go. 'They'll drag the lake. They'll try and find her, but she's not here, Crystal! She's gone!'

'Where?'

'To the other side.' Questrid began pulling her away from the water. 'Where I was! Like we both will be just as soon as we have the eye-cycle. You saw the empty chair? She's gone to the Marble Mountains.'

Her mother was free! She must be, there was no other answer.

At last Crystal found she could move. She chased after Questrid through the bent trees, over the uneven ground and down to the Town. The streets were quiet; it was early and many people had gone to the lake but things would soon be back to normal; they had to move fast.

'It's all so ugly,' Questrid said, looking around. 'And everything's broken. Why doesn't anyone move those sheets of corrugated steel? Or mend the broken windows? Or pick up the rubbish?'

'I don't know.'

'I would if I was living here. Though nothing would induce me to stay!' Questrid said.

He came to an abrupt standstill outside Grint's house and put his hand on the stone columns. 'Look at those!' he cried. 'Only a Rocker or a Stone person could make those.' He smoothed his hand over the carved stone. 'Look, there are mountains and furzz trees, snowflakes and icicles.'

'Grint made them.'

'Then he is a Rocker and he's homesick too!'

'Is he really from the Marble Mountains? I wonder why he came here?' She stared up at the empty-looking house. 'I hate this place...' She shook her head as if trying to clear her bleak thoughts. 'Now, your eye-cycle. I don't know where it's kept. Is it really so important, Questrid?'

'Yes. I don't want to let the pixicles down. And your mum is safe, I'm sure, I just need to—'

'OK. OK,' Crystal said. 'I remember hearing Grint tell Raek to put it back, but— Oh, what are you doing?'

Questrid had walked up to the front door and was turning the door handle.

'Well, I just thought it was worth a go, but it's locked.'

'Of course it is. We could try round the back.'

They crept down a narrow lane between the high garden wall and a crumbling warehouse. There were no other doors.

'We'll have to climb it,' Questrid said. 'The wall isn't very smooth, look there are footholds everywhere. It won't be hard, Crystal.'

Questrid was right and soon they had scaled the wall and were dropping down amongst the trees into Grint's garden. The ground-floor windows were shuttered. There was no sign of anyone.

'Which way?' Questrid asked.

Crystal shrugged. 'That little door was open before.' She pointed to the green door that led to the waiting room. To reach it they had to pass close to the shed where the strange animal was kept. Questrid went first and Crystal followed. She chucked down the bread and apple she'd put in her pocket as she passed it. *You can thank Questrid for that!* she thought.

The green door was not locked. They tiptoed along the corridor, pausing to listen for any sounds as they came out into the waiting room. All was silent.

'Which way?' Questrid asked as they moved into the hall where six doors confronted them and a wide staircase led upstairs.

'My first guess would be this floor,' Crystal said. 'For convenience.'

They opened each big door as quietly as they could and investigated the rooms beyond. They found Raek's laboratory, the reception room and the icy room where Grint made Crystal's mother use the eye-cycle.

'Feel it,' Crystal whispered, with a shiver. 'It's still cold.'

'I bet the eye-cycle is close by, then,' Questrid said, looking around. 'A freezer of some sort; an ice room.

Something not very large but with a big, thick door to keep the cold in.'

But despite opening every door, they could not find it. Defeated, they went back to the hall.

'Where is it? I can't give up!' Questrid cried. 'I promised the pixicles. No one but a pixicle must ever use an eye-cycle. We'd better try upstairs. But I don't think—'

'I heard something!' Crystal put her finger to her lips.

They both stood still, listening. Footsteps pattered behind the closed doors. They heard the click of a key turning. Then another.

'Quick! We must go back! Hide.'

'Stop right there!' It was Raek.

They turned and ran to the nearest door. It was locked. They ran to the next, and the next. They were all locked. They'd been trapped.

Raek came in slowly through the last door. He was swinging a big bunch of keys round and round. 'You're wasting your time. You're stuck. Trapped like flies in a jar... Who is that?' he added pointing at Questrid. 'I've never seen him before.'

'That's just Questrid. A neighbour,' said Crystal. 'Where's my mum? We were looking for Mum. She didn't drown, did she? It was a trick. I know it was a trick and you're hiding her here, aren't you?'

Questrid was impressed that Crystal had thought up the lie so quickly and distracted Raek. No one must suspect he wasn't a Towner.

'Be quiet,' Raek said. 'You're in trouble *again*, Crystal. It's a serious offence to break into Grint's house, Bless and Praise his Name! However much I try to help you, you won't help yourself.'

'You've never tried to help me! You tried to kill me!'

Raek smiled. 'No, no,' he said. 'That was an accident.'

There was a sudden bang as the front door burst open and crashed loudly against the wall.

It was Grint.

'What's going on?' he cried. 'Why is that girl here? Lock her up, Raek, her and her friend.'

'You are *so* bossy,' Raek said. '*Too* bossy.' He smiled smugly, rubbing his gloved hands together. 'I know what you're up to, Grint,' he went on. 'I know everything – the sly-ugg told me.' He turned back to Crystal. 'Grint was planning to throw me over,' he told her, 'scheming so that he and Effie could rule without me. He was going to *kill* me.'

'Rubbish!' Grint said coldly. 'If the sly-ugg said that, it was lying.'

'A sly-ugg cannot lie. It can only record and playback.'

'I'm telling you it was lying!'

'I don't believe you, Grint. You didn't know the sly-ugg was listening. It was hiding on Effie's shawl, remember?' Raek said. 'But it's irrelevant now.' He picked up a damp, cloth-covered bundle from the table. It made a soft chinking-clinking sound as it moved. 'I'm one step ahead of you, Grint. Guess what I've got!'

'The *eye-cycle!*' Questrid and Grint both spoke together. Questrid quickly forced a fit of coughing and hoped no

149

one had heard him. He stared at the damp shape. The eye-cycle was melting! How would he ever get it back to the pixicles now? What idiots these people were!

Grint laughed. 'Raek, are you mad? It has to be kept in the freezer. Look at it! It's melting. It won't work now. Don't you know what ice is?'

'I was just going to show you that I—'

'Anyway, now Effie isn't available,' Grint said, 'we're doomed. Every Sam Smith and John Carter will be after us now. We needed her! Why did you let them do that ridiculous test on her?'

'I thought it would keep them quiet. I wanted to do what they wanted.' Raek stared at his dripping bundle. 'It's only been out for a second. It can't be melting! Perhaps I'd better—'

'Too late. You're too late!' Grint cried. 'I thought you were clever, Raek! I thought you had brains!'

'I have. I do. Don't talk to me like that! Anyway, I don't care,' Raek said, changing tack. 'I hope it *doesn't* work any more. You'll be finished, Grint. Yes, you are the one who's doomed!'

Grint sat down heavily. He looked at first as if he were collapsing in defeat, but he was shaking quietly with laughter.

'The eye-cycle told me everything, Raek,' he chuckled. 'I knew this would happen. Effie saw it in a fortune. I am warned of everything and I have laid my plans accordingly...'

Raek stared at him, his mouth half open. 'What?'

'The skin on your face looks a bit sore, Raek, spotty and

red. How are your hands? I see you're hiding them with gloves. Is that because they're disintegrating, Raek? Are bits of the skin peeling off?'

Raek put down the eye-cycle and ripped off his gloves. His hands were red and swollen and horribly blistered.

'How did you know?' Raek said.

'I know about sly-uggs. It's *their* doing,' Grint told him. 'When you are mean and horrid to them, and squeeze them in your vice, they release a poison... A skin-eating poison. Have you been treating the sly-uggs *very* badly, Raek? Specially Crystal's sly-ugg? Squeezing it so tightly that it screams? Oh dear, you have, haven't you? I can tell you have. The poison gets stronger and stronger. You didn't put your face up close, did you? Oh, Raek, I think you did!' he chuckled.

Raek's hands flew to his cheeks. He cradled his face in his palms. 'Why didn't you warn me?' he cried. 'You must help me!'

'You were unkind to that sly-ugg, weren't you? You are the one that's doomed, Raek!'

Raek let out a moan like something dying and sank to his knees. 'My face!' he cried. 'My hands! Help me!'

'It's a pity Effie's gone – she could have made you a soothing poultice for your skin – while you still have some,' Grint said. 'It gets worse and worse, Raek, until you're eaten away to bare white bone.'

'No, no!' Raek cried. 'It's not true. Say it's not true. I will get better. I will!'

'Get out of my sight!'

'Please...'

'Go!'

Raek dragged himself to his feet and staggered to the door. 'I'll be back!' he gasped. 'I'll be back!'

When the door shut on Raek, Grint turned his dark eyes on Crystal and Questrid.

'So, Crystal, your mother's abandoned you. How selfish. She took her chance and has gone . . . Quickly, let's get to business. You, boy, pick up the eye-cycle and follow us!'

Grint moved fast and grabbed Crystal, wrapping his wiry fingers round her arm so she was caught tight. He pushed her towards a door and unlocked it. 'I have you. No escape. Don't even try.'

Questrid followed. What on earth is a sly-ugg? He glanced at his hands. They were fine! Sly-uggs sounded terrible! Then he forced his mind back to what was going on. He had the eye-cycle in his hands, he actually *had* it, but with each passing moment he could feel it shrinking. And the Gateway was closing; two vitally important things were disappearing minute by minute! He had to do something. He had to do something to get them out of here. The two of us against Grint is a good match, he thought. We'll overpower him. We'll do it.

He watched, waiting for his chance.

Grint locked the door behind them and pushed Crystal forward.

'The freezer is under the stairs behind some furs,' he said. 'When I open the door you put it back, boy. Just put it in and no funny business.'

'You said it wouldn't work any more!' Questrid said.

'But it might,' Grint said. 'It had lost some shape when I first found it ten years ago because it was melting in the lake water. All these years I've protected it so carefully. Foolish Raek!' He shook Crystal roughly as if she were Foolish Raek. 'So if we can save it . . . something of it, well then you, Crystal, could become the next seer . . .' Grint was clutching at straws.

He rifled though the keys to find the right one. He let go of Crystal for one second to separate the key from the others.

It was a chance. It was all they had.

Questrid shoved Grint in the small of his back. Grint let out a surprised yelp. Caught off guard he stumbled, lost his balance and toppled over, pulling a fur cape down on top of him as he fell.

'Yeowch! How dare you!'

'We dare!'

Questrid stuffed the eye-cycle down the front of his jacket and grabbed Crystal's hand. 'Run!'

24

The Thing in the Shed

There was a key in the lock of a big door close by.
Crystal turned it and they raced through. They were
back in the garden. Grint was yelling. He was seconds
behind them. Where could they go? Grint was fast. He
followed, locking the door behind him and cutting off
that exit. The only way to escape now was back
through the green door and the waiting room – or over
the wall.

'This way!' Crystal shouted. She ran towards the green
door. Questrid followed.

Somehow Grint got in front of them. He had moved
swiftly, anticipating where they'd go. He was scrabbling
with the shed door. It swung open and there was a flash of
light. Fire shot out and a patch of grass went up in flames.
A smell of scorching and ash filled the air.

Crystal screamed. 'What's that?'

Questrid stopped breathing.

Something yellow, the size of a vast sofa, charged out towards them.

'Stop them!' Grint shouted. 'Stop them!'

'It's a skweener!' Crystal cried. Her knees buckled and she fell down. 'A skweener!'

'It's a *dragon,* you mean!' Questrid yelled.

The dragon thundered towards them, its spiked wings held half-open. Anger and rage seemed to burn in its red eyes. Its flared nostrils were like the barrels of a gun, throwing out sparks and smoke.

'Get that girl!' Grint shouted again, jabbing a finger at Crystal.

The dragon bounded over to where Crystal lay in a crumpled heap. It was almost upon her, its jaws were open, and it was rearing up on its hind legs, ready to attack—

Then it stopped.

It thudded to the ground and stilled, slowly folding in its wings. The flames died from its nostrils.

'Oh, my crikey!' Questrid whispered.

Crystal wasn't even looking; she had wrapped her arms across her face. 'Help me, Questrid,' she whimpered. 'Help me.'

The dragon tossed its head. Whining and snuffling it bent down and sniffed at her.

Crystal shuddered as if she'd been burned. '*Questrid!*'

'Stop them!' Grint shouted.

Questrid was right beside her, wafting away the animal's hot breath wildly. He shook his head in amazement. 'Phew, that was close. Crystal! It recognizes you!' he cried, tugging at her. 'It's all right. Quick. Climb on! Get on its back!'

Grint was shouting, 'Get them!' and leaping around, shaking his fist. 'I'm your master. Do as I say! Eat them! Burn them! Destroy!'

Crystal dared to open her eyes and peeped nervously up at the dragon. 'I can't... I don't...'

Questrid hauled her roughly to her feet. 'They *never* forget!' he said. 'What did you do? Feed it? Befriend it? It knows you. Come on! Up. Get up!' He dragged Crystal off the ground and pushed her at the dragon. 'Come on!'

Grint let out a terrific roar and ran at them brandishing a big stick.

Questrid heaved Crystal up onto the dragon's back. 'That's it! Well done,' he said. 'Put your leg over.'

'I can't! A skweener!' She was remembering the other time, the dead skweener in the swamp. All her life she had been terrified of skweeners.

But Questrid had pushed her up and now she had one leg right over its leathery back. 'I can't.'

'You have to!'

'I—'

The dragon spun round suddenly and Crystal screamed, clutching wildly to keep hold. The dragon pounced like a puppy and puffed a black cloud of ash-laden smoke at Grint.

'Stop! Get out of— Get the— *cough cough*!'

Questrid scrambled up in front of Crystal. 'Just hold on, hold on tight,' he said. 'We're OK.' They were each lodged snugly between the protruding yellow frills that ran along the dragon's back. Questrid gripped a leathery frill in both hands. 'Up, up!' he urged it, squeezing it with his knees.

'Come on. Come on! Off we go!' There was no reason why the dragon would understand him or obey him, but that never crossed his mind. It had to.

Grint burst through the black billowing smoke and came at them again. He swung his stick but he was too late.

'Skweeeeen!' the dragon called.

Its legs bent beneath it like springs. Mighty muscles swelled and shifted beneath its leathery skin. Its wings snapped out like shutters being thrown open and began beating up and down. It rose vertically into the sky with a whooshing noise like a canvas tent flapping in a gale.

The dragon gushed out a shower of sparks over Grint. It flew up, banked sharply to the left and soared over the garden wall.

Crystal didn't scream.

She held onto Questrid's jacket. He was yelling, she could hear his voice above the *flap, flap* of the giant wings and the roar of the wind, but she couldn't distinguish the words. The dragon's pulsing muscles throbbed through her body, she heard it gurgle and roar, its lungs puffing in and out like giant bellows. It was like being a dragon herself. Never in her whole life had she been so scared. She closed her eyes as the dragon swerved and tilted and her stomach seemed to sink down to her knees. She clung tighter and dug her knees harder into the dragon's scaly skin. Next time she dared to look, the Town was tiny; far away the surrounding Wall was like a stack of toy bricks. Beyond the Wall, the colourless hills grew greener and greener in the distance.

'To Lop Lake!' Questrid cried, but either the dragon didn't understand or it had its own plan because it swooped over the rooftops and sped out towards the swamp.

'What's that great load of black stuff?' Questrid shouted. Crystal caught the tail end of his words, opened her eyes and looked down.

'Swamp!'

The dragon sank down so low it was barely skimming the treetops; any minute Questrid expected leaves to brush against his toes. Now they were directly over the swamp and slowly the dragon began to circle the black boggy ground. Backwards and forwards it flew, head swinging from left to right and right to left, searching. Crystal guessed what it was looking for. She shouted and nudged Questrid, but didn't dare release her hold to point it out to him.

Beside the broken wooden walkway, close to the tree was the image of the other skweener. There was a perfect trace of the dragon somehow cut into the surface of the swamp.

'Skween! Skweeeeen!' The dragon took one last look at the ghost of its dead mate and swerved off again, flying furiously, wildly, raggedly towards Lop Lake, crying all the while.

Questrid hadn't seen the dead dragon; he hadn't even seen the distant green hills. Every inch of him was concentrating on riding the dragon, living in the moment. I shall be a Dragon Master one day, he kept telling himself. This is what I was born for; I feel it in my bones. One day I will know everything there is to know about dragons and be famous.

He wanted the ride to go on forever and ever.

Beneath his jacket the eye-cycle slowly melted. Cold water dripped steadily down his thigh and leg but he never felt a thing.

There was still a small cluster of people around Lop Lake searching for Effie.

The dragon screeched like a banshee as it flew over the crowd and everyone turned upwards like a field of flowers turning to the sun. Each face had the same expression: open mouth, eyes wide with surprise. Then horror! The Towners' screams and yelps ripped through the air and they panicked. They ran still staring upwards, bumping into each other, knocking into the trees, stumbling over the uneven ground. Crystal thought they looked like scurrying ants and was glad they were scared. She wished the dragon would breathe smoke and ashes over their heads.

When she spotted Grint, the only one running *towards* the lake, she hoped the dragon would burn *him* to a smouldering crisp with its fiery breath.

Questrid had seen Grint too. 'He's after us,' he shouted. 'Hurry, hurry, dragon! Put us down by the lake!'

The dragon spread its wings and swooped down towards the lake as if it were going to make a crash landing, but then it veered off and began to chase the Towners. It stretched out its strong legs and pretended to grab at them with its giant cat-like claws. They screamed! Tilting sideways it dive-bombed them, showering them with ash. They hid their faces with their cloaks and yelled and screamed.

Questrid pointed at the water and shouted again. He was beginning to think they would never get down to earth, when he felt the dragon tense as if it had spotted something, or had tired of its game. It stopped teasing the Towners, changed course and with a sudden burst of speed, headed for the lake.

Really fast.

'Hang on!' Questrid yelled. 'Hang on, Crystal!'

Crystal tightened her arms around his waist.

The dragon whizzed down towards Lop Lake like a rocket. The water came up towards them alarmingly fast. The wind screamed and whined round their ears. Their hair whipped about their heads.

'We're going to crash!'

The water was *there*!

The dragon was going to *dive*!

The dragon's muscles bulged as it folded in its wings, pleating them to its side. It stretched out its neck, pushing forward, reaching... Any moment... Any moment...

Questrid shut his eyes. *Why didn't I visit my mum more often?*

They hit the water with a tremendous crack and splash.

Questrid knew immediately that it was wrong.

It was wet.

When he had passed from Pol Lake to Lop Lake, he hadn't made a splash; he hadn't felt water like this, against his skin, pushing into his ears and nose and mouth. He clamped his mouth shut against the water and closed his eyes. He was glad to feel Crystal's arms still tight around him and know she was safe. He hoped it hadn't been like this for Effie. He desperately hoped that she had got through safely to the other side.

The water was as thick as soup. They had churned up the mud, and water gurgled and roared in their ears. The dragon was trying to swim, its wings and legs were moving but they were going nowhere and it seemed the water was growing thicker and denser all the time.

They were stuck.

Stuck between the World Above and the World Below.

Questrid tried to look upwards or downwards, he wasn't sure which: it was all topsy-turvy. Chunks of ice floated slowly by. Then he caught sight of a small, bright circle. Such a tiny chink... A pinprick of light... What could it be?

The Gateway!

It was the Gateway and the dragon was trying to reach it. He was almost there. Then Questrid saw the blue glaze, the shine, and the glitter.

Ice had frozen it over.

They were too late.

25

In Between Worlds

Questrid shut his eyes again. Despite being surrounded by water, he found, somehow he could breathe. But did he want to breathe? Did he want to be alive if it meant being down here, stuck in the dark water...?

What if they couldn't even go back the other way, back to the Town?

The dragon had not given up. It puffed out like bellows, as if it were trying to blow up a giant balloon and a thunderous rumbling noise roared inside its belly.

Questrid felt it growing hotter and hotter.

The dragon opened its jaws wide.

Questrid felt Crystal hug him tighter, he wanted to speak but he couldn't open his mouth; he squeezed her hand, hoped she could feel it and wasn't as scared as he was.

A massive ball of flame, red, yellow and gold, burst out of the dragon's mouth and ripped forwards and upwards through the dirty water. Instantly the water was hot and full of bubbles. The fireball rolled through the grey and burned it out of the way so that a channel of light appeared, as if someone had unrolled a white and shining carpet for them to travel down, and the dragon spread its wings and powered forward along it. In front of them, the ball of fire glided on, burning out their path, clearing the water and ice away.

We'll do it! We'll do it! Questrid expected at any moment they would burst out into the fresh air, but now even that tiny chink of light he'd glimpsed ahead had vanished. All above was the same white colour.

All was ice.

The Gateway had completely closed.

The dragon's fireball was like a sun, a burning planet beside the wall of ice ahead. It seemed to hang suspended for an age, then there was a tremendous shattering cracking sound, as if twenty greenhouses had all exploded at the same time; a loud splintering noise and the fireball shot through.

The Gateway was blasted open.

They soared forward, forward towards blue sky and sunshine.

Crystal opened her eyes at the final explosion and saw the brilliant white and blue coming, and knew she was safe. Home!

They were moving fast, swimming or flying, it was hard to know which. Around her were melting ice and particles of dead leaf and sticks, and she saw a pale and familiar object like a fish dancing in the dragon's wake. She grabbed for it, but it was tossed aside and dragged off in the fast-moving swell. She looked back over her shoulder. 'Sly-ugg!' she cried, but the sly-ugg had vanished.

26

Home

The dragon shot out of the water like a cork popping from a bottle. It flew up, steadied itself with its outstretched wings then skidded down onto the ice, panting. Smoke billowed from its nostrils, its exhausted wings hung damply over the ice like wet dusters. Questrid and Crystal didn't move from its back but sat very still too, just breathing.

'Yahoo!' Questrid said weakly. 'We did it.'

Crystal quickly and gently removed her arms from his waist.

'Are you all right?' Questrid asked.

'Yes. Yes. I'm all right.' She turned round slowly to stare up at the smooth hills and to look at the spread of ice all around them. 'Snow,' she said. 'And ice. It's lovely. Where's Mum?' Her voice was tiny. 'It's cold,' she added with a shiver.

'We got wet,' Questrid said. 'But feel the heat inside the dragon, eh? Isn't it something!' He patted the dragon's back. 'Thanks, skweener-dragon. Thanks a lot!'

'Where do you think my mum is? I really—'

'Oh, look at the lake!' Questrid interrupted. 'Look, Crystal!'

Fresh ice was creeping between the sharp broken fragments, linking the pieces together and repairing the break. It creaked and sighed and squeaked.

'There's a face there!' Crystal cried, staring at the cloudy ice. 'Oh, no, look!'

It was Grint.

They hadn't seen him do it, but Grint had jumped into the lake after them. Without Crystal or Effie or the eye-cycle, he had chosen to leave the Town. The hole in Lop Lake was the only way home for him too.

He hammered his fist on the ice, but his movements were slow and heavy. They made no impact on the thick ice. The ice didn't even crack. His mouth opened and closed, but no sound reached them. Finally Grint slowly sank down and out of sight.

'P-p-poor Grint,' Crystal said. She was so cold her lips could hardly form words.

'Bless and Praise his Name,' added Questrid quickly. 'Isn't that what I should say?'

Crystal didn't smile. 'Do you think he'll get back all right?' she asked.

'Yeah, he'll get back to the Town, but not home. Not this time.'

Crystal shivered. 'I'm so very cold,' she said. She turned to the Glass Hills as if she were turning away from her past life and everything about it. 'I want to go home, too,' she said.

The dragon began to flap its wings gently. Inside, deep within its belly, a fire had been started up again and the warmth began to flood through its blood and skin and warm them too; their wet clothes began to steam.

Slowly the dragon rose up and flew over the Glass Hills.

Questrid felt as if he'd thrown off dirty old clothes or had a bath. The air in the Marble Mountains was so clean and sharp, so perfect. The sun was low in the sky but it was still making the snow sparkle and glitter. The purple shadows were long and beautiful. It was home.

When they flew over the last hill and the vast tree house came into view, Questrid cried out a 'Yahoo!' and this time Crystal laughed. Smoke billowed from the chimneys. Lights shone from all the windows. The place twinkled like a Christmas decoration. This really was home.

'Spindle House?' Crystal cried. 'It's even better than I'd hoped. It's wonderful! It feels so right! Will Mum be there? Please let her be there... Oh, look, a purple skweener!'

'*Dragon*. That's Boldly Seer. She belongs to the pixicles. And there are the pixicles coming out and waving their hats. And, look! Look! Your mum!'

'I see her!' cried Crystal with a sob. 'She's safe! Mum! MUM!'

The dragon skidded down through the snow and slithered to a stop beside the gate. Its body was so warm that the snow immediately melted in a circle around it. Crystal slid off its back and ran to her mother. Questrid tried not to feel a twinge of envy as they hugged. He tried not to mind when Greenwood joined them and slipped his arms round them both, circling them, bringing them all together. He knew that he would always be apart; that was how it was. When Silver came to greet him, Questrid hugged her enthusiastically, throwing his arms round her and resting his head in her shaggy fur.

'Skweeeen!' the yellow dragon cried. It spun round to face Boldy Seer, wagging its tail from side to side and showering Questrid with snow.

Boldly Seer had been watching the new dragon's arrival. She was a much larger beast, three times the size of the newcomer. She thrashed her tail from side to side and blew smoke rings. Then she ran straight at the yellow dragon. Questrid thought that she was going to attack the skweener. He cried out in alarm. But Boldy Seer stopped just before she bumped into the skweener and snorted loudly. Then she nodded her head and walked round it slowly.

They touched noses and wrapped their tails together.

'Well, look at that, I think the skweener's a *he*—' Questrid's words were drowned out by the cries of the pixicles as they rushed up to him.

'Lanky Boy! Brave boy!' they cried, tugging at his jacket. 'Have you got it? Have you brought us a present-gifty thing? A coldly-freezing one? Say you have. Say you have!'

'Look, I'm really very, very sorry,' Questrid said, undoing his jacket and taking out the damp bundle. 'It wasn't my fault. I tried but you see Raek had already got it out of the freezer and it was melting and . . .'

He laid the bundle on the snow. 'Sorry.'

The pixicles quickly unwrapped the eye-cycle. All the small protruding bits had melted away, the carving was lost; faces and figures had all melded together. The pixicles kneeled beside it as if it were a dying pet they'd been extremely fond of and stroked it sadly. 'It was a brave-courageous thing you tried, Lanky Boy,' Grampy said. 'And you have done a wonderful-clever thing to return-it back, even though it is no more use to us than an icicle hanging off a roof!'

'At least Grint can't use it either,' Questrid said.

'That is true. Very true.'

'And it wasn't that we actually needed it,' Squitcher said, 'just that we wanted it returned-back and we have it returned-back and now—'

An extraordinary noise, something between a shriek and a sigh and a laugh, made them all turn round. It was the two dragons. Boldy Seer and the skweener were snuggling down in the nest by the wall cooing at each other.

'Boldy Seer has found a mate! Our Lanky Boy has found her a boyfriend-partner at last!'

'Well, you have achieved-done something!' Grampy said. 'For many years we have been looking for a matey-friend for her. She was sick-disgusted by our choices but now she looks so blissfully-contented! Yellow must be her colour!'

Questrid was still watching the happy dragons when Greenwood came up to shake his hand. Greenwood looked different, younger somehow and with a sparkle in his eyes. 'Welcome home,' he said. 'You have done a wonderful thing for us, Questrid. Thank you. Thank you so very much.'

'It was nothing.' Questrid blushed and looked at his feet.

'It was everything,' Greenwood said solemnly. 'We will never forget it. Never.'

Effie and Crystal joined them. Someone had wrapped a thick coat round Crystal's shoulders, but she was still shivering.

'You're freezing! You must go in!' Questrid said.

'In a minute.'

'Thank you, from the bottom of my heart,' Effie said, and she kissed Questrid on the cheek. 'You risked everything for me. I'm home at last and I can live a full, proper life, thanks to you. We'll talk later, but now I must get Crystal inside. You too, Questrid, you should go in. You're all wet. Go change and get warm.'

'This place is better than the snow picture,' Crystal said through her chattering teeth. 'It's better than anything I could ever imagine. I'm so happy, you just can't imagine! The only sad thing is the sly-ugg...'

'*Sad* about a sly-ugg? What exactly is this flesh-eating sly-ugg?' Questrid asked.

'A spying slug. Ours was nice. I saw it in the water,' Crystal told her mum. 'I think it drowned.'

'Somehow it got onto my clothes,' Effie told them. 'It undid my straps so I could get out of that chair and through the Gateway—'

'And then I saw it,' Crystal said, 'as we came through but it got swept away... after all it did for us. I wanted to save it. It's so unfair.'

'Right, that's it!' Greenwood's voice was loud and

170

authoritative. 'Questrid, go and get warm dry things on. Crystal, you too. You're nearly dead with cold.'

As Questrid went into the stable he noticed the pixicles had built themselves a little ice shelter in the corner of the courtyard. He hoped they'd stay another night and he could talk to them about dragons.

Upstairs in his room he stripped off his clothes and dropped them onto the floor. As his jacket fell, he felt sure it was heavier than it should be, or maybe that was just all the water soaked in it. Then from the corner of his eye, he caught a tiny movement in the damp heap.

Questrid poked the jacket with his toe and the sly-ugg tipped out of his pocket. 'I think I know what you are,' Questrid said. He squatted down next to the strange sluggy thing. The sly-ugg swivelled its eye-stalks round to stare at him.

'Hello, Sly-ugg,' Questrid said. 'Crystal will be pleased to see you.'

The sly-ugg's orange spots had been washed away during its journey, as had its mucus coat, and it had dried to a pale greyish blue, edged with gold. Or perhaps it was cold.

Questrid didn't want his skin to blister and bubble or his fingers to fall off. He picked the sly-ugg up with his sock and let it sit on his covered palm. It felt like an ordinary (very large) slug and he had to fight back his disgust because he didn't want to offend it. 'Are you all right? I'm just using the sock, you know, because I haven't any gloves and well, what you did to Raek... Not that I'm going to torture you, of course...'

The sly-ugg was shifting slowly about. It stopped when it was facing the blank wall. It closed its eyes.

'Going to have a nap?' Questrid asked it. 'I'll just put you down then—'

But he stopped when he saw the circle of light start to glow on the wall opposite and a picture begin to appear. There were craggy mountains with thick forests growing on their slopes and pointed snowy peaks rising into the clouds. It was the Marble Mountains.

Questrid felt he was inside the image, flying through it. He skimmed over Malachite Mountain and flew past Spindle Tree House then slipped over the Glass Hills. Through a dark forest, down into a valley where a frothing white river twisted and turned he went. And there, perched on a rocky ledge, were five sly-uggs. They were waving their eye-stalks and smiling.

The sly-ugg couldn't speak, but it didn't need words. Questrid knew what he was looking at as plainly as if the sly-ugg *had* spoken.

'It's your home, isn't it?' he said. 'Your *own* home! I must tell Crystal.'

Questrid pulled on dry clothes and hurried to the kitchen, taking the sly-ugg with him.

'You've found it!' Crystal cried as soon as she saw them. 'Where was it? Or he? It must be a he or a her! Dear Sluggy,' she went on, taking the sly-ugg from Questrid tenderly. 'I'm so happy I love everything.'

Greenwood and Effie were sitting by the fire – Questrid quickly looked away when he saw they were holding hands. Greenwood with a wife! It was extraordinary.

Oriole was flitting about, twittering as she cooked. She was beaming. 'Isn't this lovely, Questrid? A full house! What a surprise it will be for the others!'

'Do you know I've even got my own room here?' Crystal told him. 'I always have had. It's right next door to Greenwood's, but it's tiny and it's only got an old cot in it!'

'Where will you sleep then?'

'I don't know. Isn't it exciting? I love this tree house. I love the way it bends and creaks. But Greenwood says there won't be room for us for ever.'

'I'll find an empty tree not far away—' Greenwood said.

'Near a lake or a river,' Effie put in.

'Yes, of course. And we'll build us a new home. A water and wood home.'

'I love the sound of that. No more curfew. No grey. No Grint. No Raek!' Crystal said. 'I am so happy! There's so much for me to find out about; so much to learn. And we'll take Sluggy home, won't we, Questrid? We'll find that place you saw.'

'Yes, we'll do that.'

And, Questrid thought, maybe I'll find a proper home for myself too. One where I truly belong.

End